JAM TOMORROW

plus eleven more

Tales of the Unsuspected

volume 2

Gwen Hullah

Published by She and the Cat's Mother

Published by She And The Cat's Mother 2024

SheAndTheCatsMother.com
Copyright Gwen Hullah 2024
All rights reserved

Earlier versions of 'Beside The Seaside', 'Jam Tomorrow', 'Would You Believe It?', 'Strategy' and 'Civility' were first published within: She And The Cat's Mother Monthly Recollections eMagazine via patreon.com/sheandthecatsmother and 'The Sharp Elbow' first published within She And The Cat's Mother newsletter/email via BrazenBitch.com

All characters in this publication are fictitious and any resemblance to real persons, living or dead, is purely coincidental. This book is sold subject to the condition that it shall not, by way of trade or otherwise, be lent, re-sold, hired out or otherwise circulated without the publisher's prior consent in any form of binding or cover other than that in which it is published and without a similar condition including this condition being imposed on the subsequent purchaser.

Book cover and interior designed by She And The Cat's Mother.
Cover image photographed by She And The Cat's Mother of
Carys Harrison's "Best In Show" at Harrogate Spring Flower Show 2019.

Paperback ISBN: 978-1-0685988-1-4 eBook ISBN: 978-1-0685988-0-7

Fiction books written by Gwen Hullah:
Safe In Killer Hands: Money, Madness, Murder
Silver Splitters: Tales of the Unsuspected
Jam Tomorrow plus eleven more Tales of the Unsuspected volume 2
The Four Seasons (complete screenplay adapted from, Safe In Killer Hands)

Non-fiction books co-written by Gwen Hullah and Ida Barker:
New Girl On The Writers' Block
Raffle Property: Your Winning Guide To House Competitions
(for entrants, property-owners and charity organisers)

CONTENTS

01. Tribute To Silence .... page 5
02. Beside the Seaside 13
03. And Then It Happened 17
04. The Prowess 57
05. Jam Tomorrow 61
06. Would You Believe It? 79
07. The Trade Off 81
08. Strategy 87
09. Blessing In Disguise 89
10. Civility 123
11. The Sharp Elbow 125
12. Don't Come Bothering Me 133

TRIBUTE TO SILENCE

She always knew that one day she would leave him. It was the favoured discard for a younger someone, which went hand in glove with dominance and the denial of gambling.

After the fashion of wives, she could always detect his winning and losing streaks from what he did not say, rather than what he did say. He would shamelessly blame her for anything or everything. She was the chilly wife, the virtuous one; always following her suspicions wherever they led. He spoke in capitals – statements – which bruised her mind like uninvited migraines.

She poured herself a cup of tea.

Himself, had been on the sunbed that very morning. He looked so tall, so blond, so orange, blatantly revelling in his reflection thrown back at himself from the saltwater glaze of her eyes. He was the type who liked to be seen; never quite late, deliberately so.

She opened her mouth to speak of the scarcity and necessities of home-life, but anger robbed her of speech, cutting through her like an old razor blade; but with the force of habit; she folded her hands in a demure manner which hid self-preservation. She imposed a quiet smile of expectancy through pale lips.

He, in the fashion of unproved husbands, knew that hopeful, hungry look, and had no intention of conforming or saving her. He found his revenge in any action would debase the value she steadfastly held onto – marriage.

He laughed – unnecessarily – then left.

Had he cared to look over his shoulder, might he have witnessed the infusion of emotions stewing; tainting her amber eyes almost black, liken to an untinned copper teapot making a poisonous brew?

She poured herself another cup of tea.

Still seated, hunched at the kitchen table, lips on the rim of her cup as she brooded over the wasted years – and how often she had toyed with possibilities which were becoming certainties. Yes. She would plan everything as simple as she could, but no simpler. After all, no-one would suspect her, a devout Christian. She smiled. Just.

With pardonable complacency, the villagers were safely anonymous to her. They saw only a fraction of her, and would probably agree they knew little of her, but plenty about him.

How could she forget over-hearing those interpret remarks while waiting so patiently in the vestry for the Chapel Officer – her confidant –

Someone said, 'Her vision is silent, quite unlike his misdemeanours...'

Someone else said, 'Quiet ones are usually dark horses. The Postmaster told me – confidentially – that she wrote fiercely, sensuous prose under a pseudonym.'

Someone other said, 'I can well believe that. I've seen the chastising way she beheaded flowers and rived out the bindweed from the "In Bloom" tubs outside The Wellington Arms...'

Then to crown it all, the organ player's voice, she recognised, had said, 'I have a loose cannon like that at home, so I can well believe and agree to the temptation of her taking a shine to – you know who...'

And they'd all laughed in a companionable way, and left the Chapel; just as her confidential friend arrived...

Still seated, sipping tepid tea, her eyes focused on the letter. The jagged edges of the envelope confirmed he had already read the written words. Reaching out for the envelope, she instinctively paused... there it was again... the inner voice reminding her there was something coming to her... she had been waiting years for it, but the feeling was too sublime, too elusive to name – she only felt it...

Feeling unquiet, she withdrew the single page from

the opened envelope. It had been folded over twice into profound creases. Pressing out the page before it could re-fold; but she had already read the words that seemed to parade upon the white sheet as though for urgent attention:

Repossession Order
No 9, West Avenue
Postlethwaite
YORK
YO1 0SE

'I am going to scream,' she told her inner-self. 'I just know it...'

She revised the plan. A sure-fire plan. There was no more need to cling onto this blighted marriage, like a ploughshare that cleaves to cold clay soil in autumn.

She rose from the table seating to put the kettle on the hob; unprepared, she caught a glimpse of herself in the mirror, and a terrible flood of revenge cascaded through her being – thinking, 'No-one would guess I was once one of the beauties of the region.' But then, she had not the slightest idea of what she was later to walk into – until she married him.

Had she chosen rather than accepted this despotic man? Who, like many men with secret lives touch people, often, and pleasantly, while secretly hating them.

Snatching the mirror from the windowsill, she hurled it into the waste bin. It cracked and splintered – 7 years bad luck flashed through her imagination, but imagination, she told herself, only encourages misunderstanding.

She brewed a fresh pot of tea.

It was when she was stirring a saccharine into the tea, she distinctly heard the sound of car wheels as they slowly turned circles on the gravel driveway; then a car door slammed shut.

Moving closer to the kitchen window, she spotted him heading towards the garage which he had selfishly converted into his study. The thinnest smile pulled at the corners of her mouth. Today, had to be the perfect day, Grand National Day – and, she had a plan. She did not have a practice of it – but just this once.

And the voice of the local conscience, if pressed, would probably say, 'She had no special skills to speak of other than crocheting squares for charity blankets.' Or – 'She's not the sort to cause a considerable stir.' And adding to gossipy, the Choral Society Members had unanimously agreed, she never hit the high notes.

A surge of anger threatened to choke her. How dare they make themselves the voice of the village conscience. They knew little of her and cared even less. She had no-one to tell her that misery had been her keeper. And now, for the first time in years the blinkers were taken from her eyes. Today, she had read more than she could stand to see. He had to leave...

He, with the certainty of, 'There will always be a tomorrow.' Jauntily, vacating his study-place with the foretaste of expectations. He headed back to his motor-car...

She, lengthened her strides, but by the time she reached his vehicle, he was already settling onto the driving seat.

Sensing her approach he turned his handsome head to glance her way. Her appearance, he noted, had the assemblance of an unmade bed, yet at the same time, aware others saw her as a faded beauty. His lips curled cruelly.

He likened her to his cold parents who had withdrawn their love. They'd wanted a daughter, instead they'd got him. A son. Consequently, they'd dressed him in frilly knickers, dresses and tied ribbons in his hair until he'd aged and was sent to boarding school. No wonder he still wet the bed when he lost.

He flinched. This dislike for them, particularly female, he nurtured close to his heart. To show his contempt, he began to wind-up the side window, deliberately, to indicate to her – her place was outside his life.

She, seeing the contempt attending his face, reinforced her intended plan. How dare he still try to blur her personality with his obscure mind-set. Incensed, she withdrew the handgun from the folds of her shabby skirt to point the barrel in alignment with his temple.

He, jerked his head to face her full on. Unshaken, he laughed loudly with the skill of long practice before raising two fingers, then slight-of-hand, placed the ignition key into the rightful place.

Provoked beyond self-preservation, she banged on the closed window with the butt of the gun. 'I hate you!' were the only words she shouted, just a fraction of time before the force of the full blast ravaged her facial features to waste.

BESIDE THE SEASIDE

This story was first published in She And The Cat's Mother Monthly Recollections eMagazine (issue number 6) April 2022 via patreon.com/sheandthecatsmother

The winter whiteness had been cold comfort for Grandma Holmes' arthritis; so, on the off chance of the weather holding-up to the promise of a forecasted warm and sunny late spring weekend, she and Grandpa agreed to treat themselves and their three grandchildren to a couple of days of pure relaxation and playfulness of building sandcastles on the excellent beaches of Scarborough;

"Just the tonic we all need," said Grandma. "Fish and chips with mushy peas eaten from newspaper wrappings while sitting on the beach smelling the fresh, salty breezes–"

Taking the pipe from between his clenched teeth, Grandpa said, "And don't forget to pack my indigestion tablets and sandals."

:

They arrived in Scarborough later than planned, due to road-works causing traffic hold-ups, causing Grandpa to perspire and curse under his breath.

"We'll have less of that gobbledegook," Grandma, alerted, glanced over her shoulder at the children, who looked hot and bothered in the enclosed space of the car.

On cue, one wanted the promised ice-cream, the other one wanted a wee-wee, and the youngest one wanted to go home.

Grandma cut through their concerns with natural patience, and handed each a bottle of fruit juices as a source of comfort...

Grandpa, tired, was driving with want of regularity, enunciated they were soon going to be running out of petrol, so they needed to keep an eye-open for a petrol station and lodgings.

Eyes bright with pursuit, Grandma, who had been looking forward to blue skies and the Maldives-palette of Scarborough waters with heightened imagination – sagely spotted a lone pedestrian walking along the cyclist lane, said, "I'll ask the man for directions to the nearest Bed and Breakfast dwelling – that should save time and petrol."

"He does look local," agreed Grandpa, slowing down to 2 miles an hour as she lowered the window. "And he does look Yorkshire. It's the flat cloth cap and the hob-nailed boots that gives him away."

"That may be so. It's also the body language of defiance," said Grandma. "I've been told, or I read it somewhere, that behind their deadpan expressions and understatements to purse-proudness, they are generous to a fault."

The flat-capped stranger readily agreed that he knew of a decent Bed and Breakfast public house that served a good bite and a clean bed, and added he would willingly come with them to give directions.

"The children won't mind budging-up to make room for you," smiled Grandma.

They did mind. And it showed.

He climbed in regardless and squeezed himself small between them, while Grandpa muttered loudly, "We'll never understand a single word he'll be saying. These Northerners flatten every damn vowel. We'll end up in Flamborough..."

After many arm waving directions and forefinger pointing, which seemed to almost amount to a detour of Scarborough, he asked Grandpa to stop driving, at the same time indicating the nearby public house – while levering himself out of the car – then, without a backward glance, he walked boldly to a terrace house, opened the front door while scrapping his boots on a fixed boot-scraper and called out, "Put the kettle on, love. I'm home..." before slamming the door shut.

Grandpa, not quite feeling – quite himself, was not scarce with mouthing rude words.

"Nana!" The children leaned forward and chorused, "What did Grandpa say?"

After a momentary reflection, Grandma said gallantly, "I'm afraid, my dears, interpretations do get lost in translations."

The children stared blankly at her.

Seeing their limits to understanding a grown-ups explanation, Grandma softened her expression. "What your Grandpa said, was, he particularly noticed the man's front door needed a new lick of paint."

AND THEN IT HAPPENED

Hugo, 40-something, still had a slight affectation to dandiness, though he sauntered rather than strutted; an unconscious throwback to his infancy and adolescent years, wherein nuisances had persistently cat-called, drawing attention to his crop of ginger hair.

Hugo did not want to remember the exact words used. He was brought up to believe emotions were self-harm; so, he had nursed his misery in silence, he believed silence was a weapon. Such exact reasoning had to be learnt the hard way, but someday, he promised himself, he would do something to amaze them all.

When Hugo reached his mid-20s he could no longer disguise the fact that he was lonely and bored with the present job within a small insurance firm which was noticeably short of single girls. Girls who laughed and chatted to other people. Being on the shy side, Hugo waited for them to make the first move. They did not.

So, acting on his inner core, he enrolled as a member of the local amateur dramatic society where he envisaged girls, if only acting, would draw him out of his shell; and there would be no telling what he or they would find.

The Playhouse Theatre's Summer Season opened to a packed audience. The play, a thriller, titled: The Lady Killer, wherein, Hugo might have anticipated – did anticipate – the supporting character part. He got one precious line within the second act bearing six measured words. He might have under-rehearsed?

'I need to write my notes,' became: 'I need to wipe my nose.' He fled from the stage through the false fireplace.

The regular audience who were avid assemblages and readers of books translated into plays, spontaneously applauded his flawed rendition; and Pru Kelp, the local journalist who reviewed the opening night, wrote a palpable column in the Friday journal, headlined: What An Exclamation.

Quote: "The highlight of the evening was when red-haired Hugo Pearson, made his first all too brief appearance on the playhouse theatre boards during the second act of The Lady Killer, a thriller. An adaption from Sheryl Westgrove's classic novel, The Mad Hatter. His sauntering entrance and sudden departure was so unexpected that it could only be described as a flash-in-the-pan performance." Unquote.

Hugo's embarrassment quickly turned into 15-minutes of notoriety. One repeated interview on television, two interviews on radio, and an invitation on a quiz show, where he was introduced to Pru Kelp, who wanted to know if his improvisation had been deliberate to get attention, or was he dyslexic?

It was her admiration for his ginger hair and his collie dog and her raucous laugh and chatty personality that had attracted him to her. The 24-years age difference did not daunt him one iota. These natural qualities she used to her advantage without a trace of self-consciousness which broadened his outlet no end. She delighted him by keeping so many sources and showbiz stories spinning at once, and he was one of them. Hugo placed himself perilously close to her. He married her.

Aspiring to a nomadic lifestyle, Hugo had caught the contagious bug of the theatricals like a fly stuck to an adhesive fly paper-tape. He could not get enough attention; so before dear old Pru decided his aspirations had expired, he vacated his day job and became a jobbing actor.

'As long as you know what you're letting yourself in for,' said Pru. 'Breaking into show-business has never been easy even if you get a toe-hold on the bottom rung of the ladder, recognition, Hugo, comes slowly – if ever – there's too many stage-players and too less outlets.'

Hugo's eyes brightened with intensity. 'Those who have no ambitions have no disappointments.' His tone accentuated the positive with the best of his intentions. 'People have always had dreams of one kind or another, and I'm aware that I'm no exception to the rule, but I'm prepared to do the donkey work, and–'

Pru had interrupted his rush of words with her raucous laugh, which had become less attractive to him since he'd left his day job at Alfred and Son's Company. 'You can say all that again,' she'd found her voice. 'Donkey work! If I remember correctly, the part you had in Macbeth which thrilled you to bits until you found out your acting part was the groaning of the dying Duncan.' She found her laugh again.

Hugo allowed a flicker of irritation to play around his lips. 'Pru, old love, after 7 years of working 9 to 5, between four walls of Alfred and Son's insurance firm, I felt like a bottle cork trapped within the confined space with the shapes of every day events of gain and loss, and after meeting you, I realised that men do require, as well as women, at least a modicum of change to seek out an out-let, to spread their wings and find happiness.'

Pru continued to nimbly top and tail a carton of red berries to make jelly jam for the summer fair. They were sat in the garden on wicker chairs, shaded beneath an apple tree.

'That's as may be,' Pru was saying, 'but pottering through repertory companies who suffer the morbid gloom of back street boarding houses' menial meals, half-empty theatres, jaded old actors; all for a pittance, I mean, after countless years of walk-on parts, being an extra and taking small supporting character roles in plays most ordinary people have never even heard of...'

Hugo stared at the red berries with insane composure.

'I think it's time, Hugo that you started to consider your life – me, after all, I shall be 60-years-old before the year is out, and I'm beginning to tire of always providing the meat while you bring home the gravy. I'm not your mother or your dog handler.'

So, wife-like, she always included his old mother and his old collie dog – now more white than red – in her references which managed to cloud the surface of their unconnected lives. Tears began to gather then pop from her eyes to drain down her nose. She did not blow her nose; wanted to look as she felt. Uncoupled.

Hugo, took a moment to digest his wife's sudden outburst of self-pity. He couldn't quite grasp what the fuss was about.

'Pru, old love, 60 is now the considered 50; you're in your prime of life, and these days people are so much more able to enrich their lives with all sorts of wonderful creative opportunities.' He reached out and took her moving hand and kissed her arthritic knuckles – thinking: I might die before her.

He nodded his head and smiled with the air of knowing sympathy – he could act. 'Bear with me, Pru, my gut feeling is that the tide is beginning to turn in my favour. This new innovating touring company I joined last month has gained a place in the Edinburgh Festival...' Hugo's eyes were bright with uncrushable purpose. 'We will all, I mean the cast, be improvising...'

'Improvising!'

'Yes, I know, it's all the rage up there. It's a monumental challenge and I'm well versed to challenges. I can well remember–'

Pru snatched her hand away. 'Remember!' Her tone had an edge to it. 'If my memory serves me correctly, I can recall the character you played in the drama, Who's Sorry Now?, who, you, was suppose to kill yourself by taking poison; who at the last minute forgot the bottle of poison, so you improvised to the walk-on extra to retrieve the bottle from the prop's room, but the guy could not find the bottle, so he came back on stage with a dud pistol and fired at you.' Pru's voice rose in frustration, 'and you fell down feignedly dead calling out: "I've been poisoned."'

There was a moment of cross-tempered silence – wherein, they weighed each other up.

Hugo was thinking: She's not kind enough for me, and I'm certain now more than ever before, she isn't the woman I'd taken her for, because she seizes my errors and uses them as a weapon. Dear old Pru is a killjoy... we're reverting even more to the people we were brought up with from birth to marriage...

He suddenly was aware of the wicker chair feeling cold beneath his weight despite the sunshine dappling through the tree foliage.

Pru's eyes darkened as she perceived the opulence of his imagined successful acting career – to be seen – burning in his eyes like glowing ember. She narrowed her eyelids to condense the years of slender income earned through repertory companies... the highlights were few and far between. The Edinburgh Festival, wherein hope reared its head – again – bringing with it the belief that a well-known producer or director could, would, should spot him, then waiting for the exclusive phone call...

She blinked the hungry years away to unexpectedly become aware of how ill-fed he looked; had she and the frugal landladies not nourished him enough? She felt a prang of guilt. Had they not exchanged vows to cherish each other till death do part... She closed her eyes, remembering the way he'd looked when he said to her: "Love me less, but for longer old girl."

:

Then the unexpected happened. A phone call from Russell Roach, the well-known producer. He'd heard through the grape vine that a musical was in the throws of being cast – auditions – in two weeks from this day of calling. The producer was very succinct. The principal part within the show, named: The Laughing Cavalier, a musical fable, was up for grabs. A powerful tragic tale, given to political satire, and Hugo was made for the part – he believed – yes. He'd spotted Hugo within the Edinburgh Festival, and noted that his improvisation grazed on satire and was achingly funny – auditions 10 a.m. to 4 p.m.

Hardly able to speak, Hugo replaced the telephone back into its cradle. He could barely contain his excitement. Dare he hope. Hope promised nothing. Hope and loss were bed-mates; he'd earned his poverty.

Hugo stared cow-eyed at the resting telephone, feeling the hairs in the back of his neck beginning to rise. Sending out intricate impulses through his body –

had he heard correctly? He needed Pru's take on this matter. She was a necessity. What she would say, did matter.

Bearing these thoughts in his excited mind, he flinched. He'd already read her inner thoughts through her darken eyes; thoughts that had reflected back at him like an automatic glass door – a stage-player, going nowhere, nowhere near the in-crowd where favouritism prevailed, and she was beginning to resent that; beginning to feel shut-out – a separateness, true, they were a vowed couple, but that didn't mean being one person. Dear old Pru thinks she knows me inside out. No. She did not. He had a secret buried deep inside himself that she had no inkling about. But one day... he would –

She interrupted his thinking, 'As a jobbing actor, Hugo, with your heightened imagination...' She had seen the terrible flare of hope in his eyes. 'It's hope that kills.'

Hugo acquiesced. He knew what that word meant to her because he knew what it meant to him, but the phone call had the smell of freshness. It had come to him in colours. He felt the need to be hosed down.

'I can well sympathise, Pru, old love.' He struggled to sound friendly, 'I mean the Edinburgh Festival was a triumph – in its own way – the Evening Post newspaper's critic reported that, "The Wilfred William's Company Show ended on festive revelry."'

'You're either in the muck, or you're in the nettles,' she murmured – perhaps intentional, perhaps not. She'd overheard the brief phone call on the extended line. 'I think we both need a brandy with ice to cool our thoughts and words... Let's pray to God that it was not a hoax call.'

:

Teatime came and went amicably enough, both sweetened by homemade scones buttered and laced with red current jelly jam. "Delicious," they agreed – after which time, Pru disappeared into the kitchen to tidy-up, leaving Hugo unable to take his eyes off the resting telephone. It was like a magnet to his senses... and yet... the face... a publicly known face had been seen, or rumoured to have been seen during the festival...

Hugo poured himself a brandy, and tried to relax. Impossible. His mind and eyes wavered into recall – hearing himself mouthing, as though from someone else's voice, an extraordinary – nah – insane eulogy; an escape from the tight reins of tether; due to sheer frustration of the make-shift backdrop unpredictably collapsing from the balustrades knocking him forwards into the fringe-cult followers' spaces, and through the blur of trousers, shorts, tanned legs and dusty trainers, he'd raised his sight and seen – or perhaps he'd imagined – the face that every stage-player would instantly recognise a mile off; but by the time he'd juddered to his feet, the sight-seer had gone...

Later, if anyone had bothered to ask him to repeat his deranged outcry, he wouldn't have known where to start. Let alone bottle it for keepsake. The drawback came when he'd arrived back and dear Pru's eyes had pinpointed the spectacular bump and the tail-ends of 8 stitches protruding from the cut-away hair close to the centre parting of his hair.

He remembered an awkward silence prevailed between them...

Pru, had been thinking – (he could read her like a script): How much longer can I put up with his inconsistencies; I'm beginning to feel as though he's deliberately crossing the road to avoid me, like he does when he sees a volunteer rattling a collection box.

He remembered smiling his practiced bohemian smile knowing she could not resist his mortar cynicism and be effected by his random behaviour which brought out the motherly protection... dear, old Pru...

But that day of all days, Pru had not reciprocated.

She was having none of it.

He had to be heard and eye-contact was necessary in this today, not in tomorrow-day. His eyes rested on his wife as she re-entered the living-room holding forth a tray with a newly brewed pot of tea with two mugs, milk jug and sugar bowl. He sagely noted the way she placed the tray carefully onto the coffee table, while saying, 'I can see you have been carrying a conversation in your head, Hugo...' Her eyes flashed undiluted knowing.

He tilted his head attractively to show his breeding – his restrain – his refulgent-self...

She was in no mood to be blinded by his brightness, her lips tightened into a creased rose bud. 'I'm use to your silences and your articulation, Hugo, and I'm immune to your foolish antics on a given occasion.' She proceeded to pour out the tea into their mugs, then sugar his – just as he liked it.

'You're a nice old wifey, really.' He leaned on that. 'I've always appreciated your grace in allowing me to follow my selfish choice of career, but you have to believe in my mission and purpose.' His eyes were brilliant, and challenging.

'When I was, err – uumph... up-skittled on the make-shift stage within The Edinburgh Festival, I simply lost the plot, but I distinctly heard your voice in my head saying, "See mistakes as opportunities" so mindfulness to the rehearsed improvisations simply passed me by completely.' He laughed, or if he did, he shouldn't have done.

Pru's expression signalled she was about to pull the damper across his draw of passion.

But he had started telling her his truth and by crikey he was going to finish his side of the happening. 'Without a word of a lie, Pru. I realised when the boards came up to meet me; I should be more like myself and stop method acting which was reducing my spontaneous nature to the likeness of refrigerated butter being spread on spelt bread, leaving gaping holes before wedged between bread sliced sandwiches for strangers.'

'No-one normal speaks so blatantly.' Her eyes scolded him, 'but you're neither normal or sane.'

She was to his eyes, so casually cruel in the name of honesty. And, Hugo had no further intentions of being a loser model. 'I felt I had nothing to lose by taking the upper hand.' He rolled the words around on his tongue as though they had flavour. 'I have no regrets, Pru. Though recollections may vary rather like speaking French, like an Englishman.'

Pru's lips outlined a shadowy smile, as she observed the man she had married, younger by 24-

years. Then he'd been on the quiet, shy side of nature. He'd worn countryside-style of suits consisting of pure wool, spoke local dialect which perfectly fitted into his natural rural surroundings...

Now, he'd changed considerably, and sometimes she felt that she did not know him anymore, though his need of freedom had not changed – needs – she silently pronounced, never vanish overnight.

Unconsciously, her glance followed his eyes to the resting telephone, seeing quiet commotion revealing itself in the uneasiness of his body language. Her glance wavered. She should allow herself to be happy for him. This was the first time he'd been importuned by a well-known producer. It was not as though he was going to leave her and old Lassie – alone – after all, auditions bring out other hopeful actors, not unlike a funeral that brings out long lost relationships – family, or otherwise, even the one's scissored-off family photographs.

'It's always an exercise to control nerves and anticipation,' Hugo was saying, between gulps of tea, 'but a result would be like sunshine.' He smiled right into her heart. 'A gift. A turning point in my unsatisfying stage career–'

'The element of surprise is crucial.' She interrupted, unable to take her eyes off him.

'Surprise! Three standing ovations...'

'It's the herd mentality of possibly not altogether safe to be around,' she murmured. Folding her arms across her breasts giving them the appearance of two suspicious strangers.

'While I staggered back onto and about the stage...' he refused to be side-lined, 'trying to make...' he grimaced, 'an effective exit, they, the audience, thought it was part of my act which caused incitement and pleasing chaos.' Suddenly, he felt dizzy and then nauseate. He could neither walk straight nor lay straight for the rest of the day.

As for dear Pru, she did not feel disposed to argue. She hushed, scolded and coaxed over him as she precariously snipped out each stitch from his cold to heated head, while blinking tears away, tears she did not know were there.

She knew how he suffered from the strive against key roles given to the favoured few – himself – the outsider, the misfit. Yet she knew, he could understand anything she could. But he felt that she'd turned away her sympathy some time ago. True. Until today. The phone call. Witnessing, again that terrible flare of hope in his clever eyes half-hidden beneath a salt and red peppered fringe... What value had praise?

The search began in earnest the very next day for sketches, bland, blatant, happy, sad, satirical, flamboyant, even the skittish takes on Shakespeare's sonnets, and down to present political affairs. They were all being selected from an old canvas back-pack stored in the loft. Keepsakes – just in case they'd come in handy one day; and this day was the day.

'A little of beyondness, Hugo, is possible,' said Pru, thumbing through the chosen ones. She paused to turn towards him, seeing him sprawled so elegantly on the sofa. It's as though, she thought, he's either re-living the lives of characters he could or should have played, but never offered, or he's re-arranging the background stage sets that he'd concocted which showed his deep resentment.

She spoke her thoughts, 'This marriage of ours has no right to work. It's become more of a workmanship arrangement.'

The words were spoken with such authority that Hugo was completely thrown. He needed a modicum of composure. He sat upright on the sofa. 'Steady on old girl, I've never cherished such unworthy thoughts, and beside that...' his voice awkwardly gentle, 'mortar cynicism does hold us together, and more-so after the unexpected phone call.' He rose from the resting place and reached for her, to kiss her with excruciating tenderness.

Pru, having acquired the nature of a wife, nevertheless, she still squirmed, enjoying the sensation with the belief of having a youthful spirit that senses the scent of expectations. Yes. It was going to be an uncloudy day, and they must let it carry them forward.

:

The night before the audition found Hugo almost unable to restrain his pent-up emotions as he strutted to-and-fro with effected strides within the bedroom space, rehearsing, then comparing to the favouritism of one of the two chosen sketches best suited to his style and timing – and he did not want to guess...

'As long as no misdemeanours rear their heads, or no ham actors encroach on your watch,' said Pru. 'And you, Hugo, do not have recourse to change your mind and recite a 5-foot pentameter instead of our finely tuned sketches that we have set our hearts on.'

Pru sat in their bed propped-up by several pillows, pen in hand, prompting, praising, criticising, coaxing, laughing, crying, talking as though she'd been asked, 'Yes. Yes, Hugo, the forerunning must be... Once In A

Blue Moon... Because it's provocative... And the alternative, Home Front which has a skittish take on social justice.' She reached for the pot of Revitalift night cream and began to apply it generously to her face and jawline.

Hugo had the advantage of standing. 'Pru, old love–' he had the eyes of a hungry canine. 'I never realised until now how passively aggressive you really are. You're stealing my excitement, and I'll have none of it–'

'Chumminess, Hugo, nearly always hovers on the verge of a squabble,' she interrupted his line of quibbles, as she smeared the night cream in circulating movements around and about her residing creases. 'I always thought of my interpose as motivation, and we both know that the most carefully prepared plans can go haywire even if one has the luxury of a recommendation.'

He collapsed exhausted between the bedclothes. 'Sorry, wifey,' he muttered. 'You're a nice old thing really despite your sharp tongue. It's just that we've never had such diverse cross words in all our years of married life.'

She screwed the lid back onto the jar of cream. 'Cross words, my dear husband, or kiss-crosses can either be used as stepping stones or weapons. If I can give and take them, so can you.'

:

The house was quiet. Too quiet. Hugo switched the radio on, just in time to hear the 5 a.m. weather forecast man voicing the day's weather forecast: 'The morning mist promise to lift and the casting clouds pose no risk of rain...'

Hugo needed to hear nothing more. He was elated despite having slept restlessly and waking with no real satisfaction. With the spirit of renewed excitement, he shouted from the bottom of the stairway, 'Wakey, wakey! It's going to be a bright, bright day,' and with that rallying call, he headed towards the kitchen to prepare breakfast, hopefully, the way dear Pru like it.

:

'Are you sure, Hugo that you do not want me to travel with you, at least, just for the company?' Pru was saying as she placed a container bearing snacks into the glove compartment of the car.

'I'll be as right as rain. I need the space, and I don't want to be pigeon-holed.' The spirit of expectation sharpened his voice and his gaze. 'When alone, I like to think that I can bring something extra to the table; beside that, dear Pru. I'm too old to be mothered.'

Her eyes searched his face, and she recognised his mission was his compass, and things would never be the same again. She felt an ache in her throat as she closed the glove compartment. He was born to leave.

Hugo, simply refused to be taken off the boil. Distraction was the last obstacle he needed. 'By my calculations, it's only 2 hours journey from here to the audition rooms held in the Provincial Hall on the outskirts of Lunmanwray,' he paused for effect, while thinking: Dear old Pru's presence would cramp my style; meanwhile I'll restore some sparkle of vitality.

Reading his thoughts through his eyes, she thought: He thinks I will put a brake on his chariot of thoughts – signposts all lead back to jazz...

A perceptive silence fell between them as they weighed each other up. Hugo was the first to break it. He spoke like a wolfish husband, cruel in the name of emphasis. 'It's a pride thing. I don't want to be seen as though I'm clutching onto my mother's apron strings. This is something I have to do alone; surely you can understand that?'

Being a fully fledged journalist, she was use to strategic withdrawals – not to see this – as a case of tactical change of plan. She smiled her professional smile with astonishingly good will, given the brevity of their relationship. After all, the phone call had been a two-sided arrangement, she did not feel inclined to argue, not wishing to leave behind an impression of ill-will. She had learned to live with his deviations, his singularity. Her eyelids half-drooped, and her mouth creased into a demure smile.

Hugo, in his own world of becoming famous – at long last – suddenly became aware of his wife's one expression, super-imposed on another, realised, too late, he had manoeuvred her into the staycation – home position. He had to save the day for his own sake – restore something to get her exercised about – then miraculously, he remembered the clash of dates; The Village Summer Fare. 'Surely you haven't forgot today is also the Women's Institute Gala, wherein you promised to arrange a stall for the Low Hanging Fruit Provisions which will also display your homemade redcurrant jelly jam..?' He had the grace and style to gather her in his arms and waltz around the cottage garden until she was quite giddy, and they toppled onto the garden bench in a disarranged huddle.

'God, love us...' She gasped, while patting her forehead with the hem of her serviceable dressing gown. 'You could turn a carrot into a peach.'

He smiled into her eyes. 'And you 10 years younger when you laugh.' He patted her arm affectively. 'I'm sorry if you felt crestfallen, Pru, by my decision to go it alone, but I'm so happy, I don't know how to share it or even show it.' He rose awkwardly from the damp bench. 'I scarcely dare to for fear of it vanishing.'

'Do not hold back, Hugo,' she swallowed her disappointment. 'All emotional tactics have a shelf-life, and we cannot afford minor illnesses.'

He grimaced. 'I feel as though I've been wrung through a wash-day's mangle, yet, this stage acting game is so damn contagious...'

'Like genital warts.'

They laughed. The relief was proportional.

'Good, bad, or indifferent,' she reasoned. 'As long as you do your best; anyway, don't the British have a reverse for something that's so bad, it's almost good.' She was now so cheerful that she was beginning to worry him; a habit that set his teeth on edge.

He squared his shoulders to give definition of his future, which restored some sparkle of eccentric gloss; the topcoat of playing the wildcard...

The early morning was beginning to turn out clear and surprisingly warm. 'No need for a coat,' said Hugo. 'I don't want to arrive at Lunmanwray in a lather.' He checked his wristwatch. 7 a.m. His eyes prowled the sky. 'If all goes to plan, this audition will be bearing roses in December.' He kissed her on both cheeks with a delicacy that seemed, to her; as unnecessary. 'No hard feelings, dear Pru?'

'How our marriage has succeeded, I'll never know, and...'

Hugo paid pleasing attention to her. 'Why our marriage has lasted for so long, old girl, is because we're both in love with the same man.'

She raised her eyebrows. 'There are somethings that only belong to women.'

Impatient to take his leave, he placed a tentative arm along her shoulders. 'You are a wickedly, wonderful person, but I must love and leave you...'

'Yes.' She could not say less, feeling something different was about to happen before the day was out – then – the feeling was of little moment.

:

The rhythmic sound of the car tyres on the hard surface of the motorway leading towards Lunmanwray town matched the luxury of Hugo's moods. He was buoyant with anticipation and excitement at the promise of success within his grasp; something to hold onto – to awaken and receive warmth from. He settled back in the driver's seat; a happy man. It had been all grist to the mill. All that grinding to the mechanics of theatrical shaftings...

He rechecked his watch. 8:45 a.m.; didn't want to appear too eager or too early, but not too late as to be not noticed. Winding down the window to let a soft breeze waft into the car, he raised his sight just in time to see a large warning sign erected on a concrete post beside the roadside:

NEXT SERVICES STATION
36 MILES

Hugo inclined his head graciously, Pru, he knew, had thoughtfully placed a container bearing 5 litres of petrol within the car boot. Feeling elevated, he eased his foot off the accelerator peddle and relaxed.

Then it happened. The car stalled, and with it, his heightened sense of euphoria evaporated. He was brought back to the austere aspects of reality.

He restarted the engine. It spluttered dully, then wheezed into silence. Baffled, he vacated the vehicle to lift the bonnet and peer onto the mechanics... 'Surely not the battery,' he muttered helplessly because to his understanding; it would have recharged itself due to the length of his journey.

He rechecked his watch. 9:10 a.m. Audition schedule 10 a.m. to 4 p.m., and he was no mechanic – and the next service station, he calculated – could be 12 to 15 miles away. Returning into the vehicle, he turned the key – hopefully – to restart the engine – to no avail. A flicker of irritation played around his mouth as he automatically felt within his trouser pockets for his mobile phone.

'Damn!' He remembered that he'd placed it into his jacket pocket. His eyes glazed into recall...

Pru had handed to him his jacket, and he'd waved it aside saying – 'No need for a coat today,' because the weatherman had announced – had stated – the day promised to be sunny throughout.

'Just in case you go off the boil,' she'd said, '... or the phone call was a hoax.'

Beads of perspiration, he could feel, were beginning to form on his forehead, and on the roots of his hair. All at once he became aware of the currents of draughts from speeding vehicles as they drove by at seemingly dangerous speeds with a view to overtake. A waver of uncertainty beckoned his next move. He squared his shoulders. 'I must sweat the small things,' he reasoned sanely. 'Small things can create big things, and I must not tempt providence. I must man-up. Not act-up. I must push the car into the hard-shoulder on the motorway, trap a telling note under the window-wipers, lock the doors, then cadge a lift to the next petrol station and enquire about a breakdown service...'

:

2 hours later, feeling as though he'd been wheeled too close to a fire-grate, Hugo alighted from a transit van with a delicacy that looked unnecessary if anyone had cared to notice. They did not.

The service station was short staffed, to the point of being cross-tempered, and the breakdown vehicle with driver, would be back on duty anytime soon...

After consuming three cups of coffee the driver and breakdown vehicle arrived to transport him back to the whereabouts of his abandoned car; to find that two front wheels had been stolen, and the driver's door had been forced open – radio removed along with Hugo's lunchbox. And, to add insult to injury, a thank-you note was left on the passenger's seat, thanking the car's owner for the £40 – in cash – enveloped in the food-box.

Hugo could only think of one thing – audition!

'Audacious,' agreed the driver, which signalled

brotherhood of human misunderstanding, followed quickly by the want of a decision – to load-up or not?

Feeling at the mercy of his emotions, Hugo felt obliged to knuckle down to daily manual work, which he'd always kept at a respectable distance, but today of all days, needs must be framed accordingly. Using the breakdown man's mobile phone, Hugo rang home.

The answer phone was switched on. Yet no reply. Hugo cursed under his breath. He should have remembered, Pru would be on the village green attending to The Women's Institute Stall.

In desperation, he rang through to Pru's place of work, The Daily Paper, to confirm who he was and her status there, and after impatiently hobnobbing with others – finally – he was put through to the accounts department.

Yes, the cost would be deducted – as usual – from Pru Kelp's wage account, and yes, the breakdown's proprietor costs would be honoured, as they detected nothing that needed avoiding, which included a taxi to take him there and back from the audition.

'Sorted!' said Hugo, smoothing down his damp hair, aware of the driver hovering close enough to hear the arrangements.

'Sorted,' agreed the other, with a smile and an outreaching hand to collect a handshake. Names and addresses were exchanged.

Meanwhile, the desk assistant phoned a taxi rank... 'A taxi would be arriving in approximately 20 minutes.'

Pulling into the service station, Hugo rechecked his watch. 2:50 p.m. His mind was on fire. He made gestures of defiance... thinking... 3:10 p.m. Less than an hour before the deadline. He forced an imperfect smile through dry lips, and commonised his accent when enquiring where the latrine and washroom was situated.

Standing to attention in front of the community toilet mirror within a scullery sized room dignified as the washroom, Hugo refused to be surprised by the dishevelled image of himself reflected back at him; hair askew, a shave was needed, oil stains on his shirt and trousers required attention. Improvisation was the key to his salvation. He ducked his noble head beneath the cold tap and turned it on full blast. The shock was beneficial, then mercifully dried off with sheets of toilet paper before turning shirt inside out, then raking his fingers through his hair.

Taking a step backwards, he stared back at himself in the mirror, noticing, shamelessly, his amber flecked eyes had a tiger-ish intensity of feelings, surely, The Laughing Cavalier character would resemble such a roguery appearance – such was the depth of his feelings, he spontaneously began to recite, Once In A Blue Moon.

Seated back at the same table where he'd taken ownership because of the view to the forecourt, Hugo sat agitated, making a cup of coffee and a packet of bacon scratchings last for well past 3 p.m., without sight or sound of a taxi arriving – until – 3:16 p.m.

Seditiously, before the vehicle wheels stopped turning, Hugo opened the side-door and head-butted his way onto the passenger seat, while enunciating, 'To save my sanity, will you please drive with urgency – please!'

In no mood to cleanse his words – words directed at the unsuspected road closure, due to roadworks – the taxi driver, like others, took a diversion route leading into Lunmanwray town; adding an extra twelve miles to the journey – robbing Hugo of precious time.

:

2 minutes to 4 p.m. – Hugo stood perspiring, cursing, as he faced the entrance closed door, thinking, a knock would hardly be sufficient to open it and his rundown appearance would surely undermined his status. He tried the door handle. The door was locked from the inside to any outsider. Pounding the door, which he

could not help noticing needed a new coat of paint – then – what seemed like an eternity, two bolts scrapped back into their brackets before the door was opened, and a man wearing an unmoveable expression stood before him.

'I'm Hugo Pearson,' he announced grandly.

The man's eyes raked Hugo's appearance, from dishevelled damp hair surrounding a red perspiring face to the dusty footwear. 'Sorry, I did not not catch your name,' his eye wavered into vagueness.

Hugo reintroduced himself, his voice awfully self-sufficient upper-class, yet, flirtatious; all to no avail.

'If you're here looking for scrap iron or indeed shelter, then you're looking in the wrong place.'

Hugo was even more acutely aware that his shabby appearance disqualified a decent conversation or opinion, but his future was at stake, he must not show or lose his temper. After all, this pious individual may well be a director of, The Laughing Cavalier musical show, therefore, he must apply dignity laced with charisma...

'I'm here as requested by Russell Roach, the producer of, The Laughing Cavalier. He personally rang me at my home address requesting my presence here at the audition rooms.' He smiled into the other's unmoved face. 'Mr Roach saw my performance in the

Edinburgh Festival, and–'

The chilly doorman interrupted with precision, 'The producer, Russell Roach left this building approximately...' he side glanced his watch, '8 minutes ago.'

'Left!'

'Yes. Left.'

'He cannot have left. He knew I would honour his phone call. I'm a reliable stage actor of high regard in the province areas. I'm...' A flashback suddenly affected his mind's eye – The Ham; the main actor, standing centre stage demanding his servant – him – to pour out a glass of brandy – instead – he had handed the over-bearing actor a glass urinal containing urine. The audience had laughed – followed by a ripple of applause. He was sacked. Hugo blinked the image away; pronouncing the hazards that he had to overcome simply to arrive here on the doorstep...

The doorman raised his hands, the inner part facing Hugo, and for a wild moment the thwart actor thought the man was going to strike him.

'I have no appetite for your bullish attitude, so please leave these premises, at once.' He made a positive move to close the door...

Hugo rammed his foot onto the doorsill to prevent the closure.

The doorkeeper stared back at him in a cold untraceable way. His lips curled like a pig eating a strawberry. 'Just make yourself scarce, and make do with left-over...'

Unable to rein in his inner misery and rage, without further thought, Hugo raised his arm, and with a clenched fist brought it down upon the other man's bulbous nose. He had the satisfaction of seeing the supercilious man's demeanour change to surprise, and the penalty result – an excruciating yelp of pain. The door slammed shut.

:

Pru, was in the kitchen. She looked anxiously at the wall clock. 10 to 8 p.m. Still no sight or sound from Hugo. She rechecked the dinner cooking slowly in the oven which she had prepared with loving care to celebrate his return with good results. No-one deserved success more than Hugo Pearson.

It was while Pru was – again – rechecking their special meal; all beginning to look over-cooked in their co-ordinating oven-proof dishes, when she heard the sound of a vehicle arriving – not, she perceived, the familiar grinding of gears and the blowing of a car horn heralding he was home. She felt a shiver of alarm as she turned the heat down low; did not want the special meal to dry out, she hastily went outside, in time to see Hugo stepping out of a taxi, with the familiar body language of rejection. Her heart sank. He'd been thrown to the wolves again.

Wifely, she poured him a stiff measure of brandy. 'Just to get you off the ground, my dear.' She made a move to put her arms around him.

He brushed her aside as a vexed Mother does to a demanding child. He gulped down the spirit without appearing to taste the drink, then, refilled his glass to the brim.

'Dinner is ready if you're hungry, if not, it will keep for later.' She spoke with careful impartiality. She knew through experience, how not to antagonise a man in civil discord. She bit her tongue.

'Don't fuss! I'm not hungry!' He spoke abruptly. 'I need space to work my way around this... this...' Finding the right word seemed impossible. He turned on his heel, left the kitchen, and headed for the treehouse – his study – which he'd constructed years ago in the cottage garden.

Leaving Pru thinking: It's so sad to see the back of someone you love.

Refreshing the teapot, Pru poured herself a cup of tea, then made her way to sit down, to finish writing her latest review in time to meet the newspaper's deadline. The sound of the house telephone broke into her troubled thoughts. She rose from the kitchen chair and headed for the living-room for the first time in the day, to see the red light flashing, notifying a recorded message... a cold-call, she decided. But she was in no mood to answer to a stranger... yet...

Lifting the receiver, she was surprised to hear an unfamiliar voice stating, 'I'm Russell Roach's secretary, Laura Armstrong, calling from Lunmanwray. I believe that I've been given the correct telephone number...' A pen nib could be heard scrapping over paper... 'if so, may I enquire has Hugo arrived back to his digs? I know it's rather late in the evening, but this call is urgent.'

Pru acquiesced, to give herself time to think. She could hardly reveal that a grown man was sulking in his treehouse in their cottage garden. 'Not yet, Laura, but I'm expecting my husband to be home anytime soon, so I'm more than happy to take your message for him, and...'

'Mr Roach, eventually heard of Hugo's unforeseen delays and his genuine strife to arrive at the audition rooms today on time, and also the unfortunate assault on the doorkeeper, Roald, who answered the banging and shouting on and at the locked-down entrance door, to a so-called actor, called Hugo – someone or another, from the Edinburgh Festival...'

'Assault?'

'Broken nose.'

'Broken toes?'

'Nose, or as some would say, snozzle.' Having made her point, she went silent.

In the manner of a dutiful wife, Pru broke the silence archly. 'Really, that does not sound remotely like Hugo, he's gentle as Mary's lamb. No – no, he's a true gentleman, he's–'

Laura interrupted sharply. She'd had her belly full of out-of-work actors bending over backwards to challenge Judges' decisions. Not to mention giving her their well-thumbed bin-able CVs. 'The doorkeeper, Roland, err – Ronald, has been pacified with the offer of an exiguous part in our project, The Laughing Cavalier musical show, so that's one less problem to solve.

Laura's words focussed Pru's mind like sausages spitting in a hot frying pan. 'A little bit of beyondness,' suggested Pru, holding onto herself, 'can go a long way, Laura.'

'Yes. Mr Roach had taken a shine to Hugo's acting abilities within the festival and he's still interested...' she paused. And the sound of turning diary pages travelled down the line. 'He has a free afternoon this Wednesday. 2:30 p.m. to 4 p.m. to enable an interview with Hugo, so please forward this message.'

'He'll be there, I promise you, even if I have to wheel-barrow him there.'

Laura, had the grace to laugh, quietly. 'I'll leave you to follow through the proposal. Good luck.' She rang off.

The horizontal rays of the evening sun cast shadows of farewell to the day, as Pru stepped into the garden. 'Come on, Lassie, let's find Hugo.' She coaxed the aged collie dog. 'Come on, let's high-jack he who thinks absurdity is more effective and more fun.'

Lassie wagged her tail in response to her articulate sounds, despite being deaf in one ear, and her arthritic hind legs which gave her an irregular gait.

Pacing her strides to coincide with her pet's measured tread, Pru paused here and there de-heading flowers, thinking – until Hugo had come into her life, by fault and stayed on purpose, she'd devoted herself to journalism... yet, there was no resemblance between them. At first she'd pushed him aside like peas on her plate. His closeness had been too overbearing, but in the end, it all came down to soul, and you cannot fake that... which brought her mind strictly back to the urgent phone call.

'Come along, Lassie,' she spoke aloud to catch their house-pet's attention. 'Let's find the child-man, rouse him from his bolt-hole...' she paused for Lassie to catch up to her, while casting anxious eyes towards the beech tree that housed his thoughts and studies of one play after another, and as she came closer to the treehouse, she could see that several lower rungs of the ladder stairway were broken. Was that evidence of arrival or departure? She asked herself. Was he in-house or outside? She decided to walk around the tree to give herself further reflection – Had he accidently fallen from the treehouse, after all, he had had a glass of brandy on his return home, followed by helping himself to a generous second refill, perhaps he was laid concussed; and she was no nurse.

Lengthening her stride she rounded the tree, and what she witnessed rooted her to the ground. There camouflaged in the armoury of the dappled evening sunrays penetrating through the tree branches and their foliage, stood Hugo, balancing unsteadily on the platform of their portable step-ladder with noose round his neck – from a rope secured around a higher branch.

'Don't... don't!' she shouted. 'Russell Roach has just phoned... he...'

'Wh – a – t!' His voice was discordant.

She nodded wildly. 'Wed-nes-day!'

'Wedd-in-day,' he pronounced hoarsely.

'Aft-er-noon!' Dear Pru raised her eyes to help meet his downcast eyes. She shivered, sensing the disconnection. 'Ap-point-ment!' Painfully she swallowed her dread – was this really happening... or were they caught in a nightmare?

'Ap-point-ment.' The word was difficult for him to pronounce, as it was to hear it.

She waved her arms frantically into the air, perceiving a terrible flare of hope. And it's hope that kills you, she thought dementedly. 'Yes – yes...' Tears popped out of her eyes and rolled down her white cheeks to rest briefly upon her moving lips before dissolving saltily in her mouth. Dear Pru, was at the mercy of her emotions.

He could not bear to look at her any longer. Her misery was his misery. He reached upwards as though to undo the knot in the noose... his feet wavered...

She screamed and once she'd started to scream – she could not stop.

Lassie hearing the shrill sounds came running awkwardly towards the commotion wagging her tail excitedly in spite of ailments, but she came panting alongside Pru and licked her clenched hands, then, sensing the scent of Hugo – her master – she barked happily at his whereabouts by jumping onto the two lower steps on the step-ladder and at the same time, raising a front paw in obedience to the learned handshake.

Hugo, feeling the jolt coming from the bottom of the step-ladder, leaned precariously over the top bar...

Lassie's instinct to the sudden unsteady movements – jumped clumsily off the household apparatus, knocking the step-ladder from beneath her master's feet...

THE PROWESS

A young woman with an old face; a steely eyed young woman with prematurely silver hair, wearing a dark tracksuit matched with a cross-body strap holdall; strolled along the high street.

She turned from the main street to walk along Harper Avenue; pale eyes turning almost black with intensity of feelings as she scanned each pre-war house in turn before halting briefly before number 23; a substantial house which suggested the owner employed a housekeeper and an odd-jobbing person for the upkeep.

Casually, she opened the railed gate to leave the sneck unconnected to its bracket before proceeding along the flag-stoned path bordered with geraniums, ground-covering roses and ornate cabbage plants.

A quiet smile of expectancy escaped through pale lips – any pedestrian passing by, if asked, would have thought from her appearance, she looked like a cleaner or a leaflet distributor.

She knocked twice on the front door. The door remained closed. Turning away, she strolled round the house to knock upon a side-door while leaning in as though listening for inner sounds – then, lifting a nearby plant pot bearing an abundance of blooms, to take a key. Nimbly, she inserted it into the lock; movements all done in a narrow strip of shadow from a near-side pine tree; she entered the house, to close the door with familiarity, to place and turn the key within the inside lock.

Entering the hallway where a grandfather clock stood ticking unretrievable time away, she paused briefly, before easing the towering clock aside to reveal a small cubbyhole – wherein, the exiguous space, two rows of tarnished ornaments were aligned; all sizes and shapes. With interested eyes she selected several items and placed them onto the side-table. Automatically she took from the copious holdall a can of cleaning substance and a clean cloth. Giving the container a brisk shake before unscrewing the cap to press the fixed sponge against each ornament, in sequence, followed by a brisk polish; all done with expertise to reveal the shine of silver.

So intense was her pleasure that she was lost in the moment of admiration of the silversmith. It was the grandfather clock striking the hour – 3 p.m. – closely followed by the knocking on the side-door, to the sound of the door handle being force-turned. Wasting no time, she gathered the silverware and placed them into her holdall with the skill of long practice, while listening intently to the footsteps leaving before unlocking the door and stepping outside. Rounding the corner of the house she caught the glimpse of a big respectable man – at least that's how he seemed until he spoke. The voice had an almost fatal carrying quality.

'I'm here because Mr Arkwright enquired about Prudential Property Locksmiths installing burglary safety alarms and locks.' His careful eyes suddenly pinpointed her bulging cross-body strapped holdall.

Without batting an eyelid, she coolly met his want of knowing with an exquisite smile, and said, 'A weekend away.'

JAM TOMORROW

This story was first published in She And The Cat's Mother Monthly Recollections eMagazine (issue number 10) September 2022 via patreon.com/sheandthecatsmother

Della took off her earrings as she reached to answer the telephone. 'Hello, Della Ware speaking...' she paused. 'Oh, it's you, Arthur darling...'

Pause.

'Yes, but at the moment I've nothing to add...'

Pause.

'I understand perfectly, Arthur, and the idea is quite awful...'

Pause.

'But I need time to consider,' she replied in a distracting way, 'it's just that I'm tired of pretending to be happy when I feel rather tepid...'

Longer pause.

'Not yet, I need time to reconsider the fullness of...'

Pause.

'I hear what you're trying to tell me, Arthur, but it's probably the dampness hovering here in the house that's so toxic.'

Della looked across the room at her old mother. They shared a conspiratorial look. On cue, the old woman broke into an asthmatic cough which wheezed its way down the telephone line...

Pause.

'I know... I know...' Della hoped her sympathy – wanted her sympathy to sound persuasive, 'that's why I'm hesitating so much over your proposal, simply because I'd be worried sick in case Mummy couldn't cope here on her own,' she lilted her voice, 'I mean – two open windows and a cross-draft chills her to the marrow.'

Pause.

'Not tonight, darling – tomorrow – usual place. Goodnight.' Della replaced the receiver back into its cradle, then lowered herself back onto the hassock to face her mother, who sat rigid, holding a skein of wool – widely – between her thumbs and two rows of arthritic fingers; whose ears had been strained to make sense of the inaudible sounds coming from the caller – Arthur Appleby.

Della picked up the half-finished ball of wool she had been winding...

Her mother automatically began to sway her hands sideways to the rhythm of her daughter's, coiling the spun threads of yarn into a neat ball.

'Arthur won't change his mind,' said Della.

'Then you'll have to change it for him.'

'Easier said than done. He's not easily persuaded. He's so set in his ways.'

An expression of solid metal spread across her mother's face. 'Then you'll have to make yourself more available – more sexually attractive, my girl. We're behind with the mortgage, and the utility bills are mounting up and already the damp has shown its toxic presence from behind the skirting boards, and you've had to dampen down the fire with ashes to make it last longer because we can't afford the extra bag of coal.' She shuddered, blinking back the tears she didn't know were there... 'And don't you dare not marry that sugar daddy, everyone knows he's not short of brass.'

'And everyone knows he's a confirmed bachelor and they'll be surprised if he succumbs to marriage.' Della's eyes were brilliant with expectations.

'A man who doesn't understand women doesn't want to understand women–' Her mother's face glistened with exertion.

'Perhaps that's a good sign in the long run,' interrupted Della optimistically.

'And men who understand women, so often understand too many women, and I know all about that!' The tears dried on her hot, creased cheeks.

Della reached out and patted her mother's swollen knee, aware of the magnetic patella that supposedly eased her joint pain, while unintentionally lowering her eyes to the passive leg exerciser's foot plates gliding silently back and forth, which mercifully aided her to daily exercise her beloved Jack Russel.

'Arthur said with real passion that he doesn't want you or your snappy dog living under his roof, if and when we marry.'

'But we wouldn't be under his feet.' Her mother's eyes widened and her mouth tightened. 'There must be over 12 rooms in his big house that's surrounded by acres of manicured lawns...' She paused in speech as her house-pet companion appeared from beneath her easy chair, ears alert, wagging its stub tail before shaking itself down with vigour and heading for its water bowl.

'Such a prevaricator.' The old woman's careful eyes rested on her daughter's homely face. 'Are you sure you can handle such a selfish man? A man who to me suggests the presence of another kind of artificiality,' she murmured spitefully.

'You are a wicked old woman,' Della said without malice, handing over the completed ball of wool.

Her mother impatiently dropped it into a canvas tote bag. 'At my age, I'm entitled to be.' She reached out for the tin of broken biscuits and prised the lid open. 'It's not as if I was stone deaf, incontinent or can't climb the stairs without a bannister rail. And I don't need a home help to bath me every day, and I can still string sentences together without being uninteresting despite his sarcasm, and you know as well as I do that I can still whip up a decent Yorkshire pudding.'

Della didn't know whether to laugh or cry; remembering how her mummy – sometime ago – had a fundamental sunny-side and a positive outlook to life, but now she was consumed by their circumstances and the want of necessities and comforts of life. There was no getting away from the feeling that she was emotionally tied to her umbilically; as for Arthur, he had to be the solution to their dilemma. Suddenly an obscure idea struck her far from promising and was possibly appalling, but, she told herself, the impossible becomes possible.

:

The wedding was held in the town's Register Office – quietly – Arthur's accountant and his chauffeur, including the resident cleaner attended the service. Arthur's parents had long gone; he being the only child – the rooster – of the family haulage business, so naturally he'd inherited lock, stock and barrel, but as yet, no heritor. Della, he secretly hoped, would serve his purpose – a family benefactor – and comfort in his retirement.

:

Meanwhile, Della's mother sat like a titled Dowager on a personally selected high chair in Evergreen; an old people's private home. After the first shock, followed by gallant recovery, Della's mother had conceded to her daughter's unnerving plan. A plan with promising luck that somehow her only child had coaxed out of their dismal circumstances.

'As long as you don't go off the boil, my girl,' she'd said, as she set foot over the entrance steps of the old people's home. 'I trust this is a short-term stay, because I don't want to be left here on my own. I'll have no-one to come to my funeral.'

'Trust me, Mummy...' Della's eyes were bold with purpose, 'you'll not end up in a pauper's grave. Arthur's desperate for an heir to take on his family business, and I'm not menopausal which I half believe was my attraction in the first place, after all, Arthur hasn't had many useful lovers, and no illegitimate children which must feed his needs–'

'And what about your feelings for this old despotic man?' interrupted her mother with reverence, she could act.

Della's laugh was unnecessarily loud. 'Oh, I'm fond of him in my own way. He's clean. Obedient in bed – relatively – but top of my list is security and to bury the roots of fractures and heartbreaks.'

'And what about me? Do I still come into the picture?' Her daughter had the grace to stop laughing.

'When I say to him that you're really a nice old thing and I'm sure he would like you once he got use to you, he'll say – "Who?"'

'Piggafrogary,' murmured her mother with flexible dignity; remembering he'd acknowledged her with a monthly cheque payable to the old people's home.

:

6 months later, as promised, Della visited her mother before checking on Rufus installed in nearby kennels each day; bringing with her delicious treats which her mother had never set eyes on in her whole life. 'Does Arthur know of these affordable gifts?' She would smile, laugh and gesture out of all proportions. She had taken to vaping.

Della, refreshed and triumphantly pregnant would say – 'Not so much that I would notice. He's more constrained, more concerned about our expected baby's arrival. He won't want to rock the boat.'

'He's distracted as we all are.' Her mother could eat and talk at the same time. 'It's only the blessed that can be so easily ungrateful.'

:

Then, the unthinkable happened. It was while Della was visiting her mother and taking Rufus back to the kennels, when Arthur decided to prune the grape vines in the orangery to fill in the intermittent gap, while his wife returned from her daily visits. She knew her own mind, he'd discovered with unease, and imposed it with spirit which disturbed and worried him no end.

Arthur's mind began to dwell – again – upon the cost of keeping her cantankerous old mother and her infernal dog both residing in luxury they really were not accustomed to, and how his pregnant wife was driving 20 miles each day to accommodate their needs in the heat of summer – returning home to attend to unnecessary housewife jobs, like moving furniture from one room to another, despite him having employed a housekeeper for years... surely that would begin to tell on her health, and his inner happiness, but he didn't know how to show it, feared to show it in case he incited fate or even a divorce.

Uneasily, he thought about his own childhood – of his own lonely upbringing – his chilly parents. They had been so busy, always working, 'Time is money!' they would say –

And he would plead, 'But I'm here, I'm not invisible.' Arthur swallowed his anger of never been able to forgive them for withdrawing their love from him. He blotted the sweat from his brow with his shirt cuff, and moved a step higher on the ladder to eye a rogue branch bearing little fruit, which brought his mind back to Della's mother...

Arthur checked his watch again with a sudden prang of guilt because Della's old mother was in an old improved folk's home instead of the conservatory or the spare rooms, which he knew Della was secretly arranging for her mother to accommodate – eventually – and when he'd hinted that he knew her way of thinking, she'd replied, 'It cuts both ways, Arthur, because sometimes you're like a suspicious stranger to me, and that's not good for the baby.'

Arthur blinked the alien image away. He could hardly believe he was married, let alone heading for fatherhood. He felt an inward flutter of pain – was it happiness? Steadying himself on the step-ladder, Arthur's mind dwelt transiently on how this woman – his wife – who had, morning and night diligently – or so it had felt to him, folded him in her arms before pushing him through a mangle machine to wring him out dry, all under the heading of parenthood. Arthur broke out in a second terrible sweat... Would his heart stand up to such a life pattern of intense passion?

He rechecked his watch. 40 minutes to 7. Della would now be returning the old woman's dog back to the kennels before driving the ten miles back home in the summer heat. Again, he wiped sweat from his brow with his shirt cuff. What if she felt nauseous of fainted at the wheel – became involved in a road accident – caused an accident enough to induce a miscarriage? So tense was his feelings, he unconsciously over-reached for the rogue vine branch by over-stepping the top platform of the ladder, to flounder dangerously before falling backwards to find himself staring up at the roof skylights, dimly aware he was thrashing away amongst broken terracotta jars, over-turned geranium pots, all tangled between dislodged vine branches and a collapsed ladder. His natural reaction was to struggle to his feet. It was impossible. The pain in his chest and lower body was excruciatingly painful, too painful to bear. Mercifully, he blacked out...

:

Della found Arthur, later, lying at mercy amongst the debris – semi-conscious – 'Arthur, what have you been playing at?' she shouted, hoping he would hear her, 'your housekeeper has contacted your family doctor and an ambulance should be on its way sometime soon.'

Arthur half-opened blood-shot eyes ablaze with pain to take in her presence, hoping not an apparition. 'Oh, Della. Old girl...' his diction was barely audible. 'I need help.' (He'd never needed help before). He raised a limp hand to gesture where the terrible pain was in his body. 'And I've never been so glad to see you.' His lips twisted into a regardful smile.

Della smiled because he recognised her. She lowered herself onto an up-turned flower pot. 'I can't even begin to imagine how I'll be able to nurse you day in and day out as well as visiting Mummy and Rufus every day, especially in this summer heat...' her voice caught in her throat. 'No wonder the baby has started to kick...' she paused for breath. Arthur held his breath.

He looked at her through pained eyes, seeing her rosy, hot complexion. He flinched. She looked tired. Even in his appalling state, he sensed a circumstance which was far from promising and was possibly damning, but he must take the lead and man-up. Arthur cleared his throat and heard his own words forming the answer to the obvious solution. 'Why don't we invited your mother to stay and...' he lapsed momentarily remembering the first time he'd called at the old woman's house to pick-up Della, and the aggressive little dog with its hair bristling erect had barked its head off before cocking a hind leg up to urinate against his trouser leg. He'd hated it from that day on. An expletive escaped his parched lips... he masked it with a genuine groan. Just.

'And Rufus.' Della's bright eyes brimmed with tears, exuding that brand of good fortune, her lips curved upwards in an expression of perpetual happiness. 'Oh, Arthur, you darling man.' She rose from the flower pot to raise his head upon a cluster of wilted geraniums, then kissed him so tenderly upon his creased brow and in such an exquisite way that he felt as though she was bringing on a gentle and easy death, to end his suffering.

'Oh, Della,' he whispered in a low hissing sound. He'd never felt such peace before because nobody had wanted him much or cared whether he was present or not... 'Oh, Della, stay with me... I do love you.'

And from a far distance he heard her say: 'Arthur Appleby, you do say things without much thought, just to get a reaction.'

Awash with pain, Arthur could only hope she

wouldn't ask him to repeat or spell out those hard to say words.

Afterwards Arthur couldn't remember making such an obvious remark.

:

'Poor Arthur,' said Della pouring out tea from a large stoneware teapot as her mother entered the orangery pushing a hostess tea trolley bearing sensual gratification. 'Four cracked ribs and a broken hip joint, but I've been assured that he'll rally round–'

'Rally?'

'The doctor said at his age, 3 score years and 10–'

'74,' corrected the old woman. 'It's no wonder he fell from the ladder.' She looked her daughter in the eye. 'When you told me yesterday about his accident, my first thought was that it was wasted on him, I mean...' She squeezed herself small onto an antique chair which wasn't meant for someone so ample. 'Ribs and only one hip. My second thought was...'

'I think a lot of thoughts would be better left unsaid.' Della reached out for a crustless sandwich. She bit deeply into it then tongued it aside. 'Words spoken can't be taken back and they can be used against you as weapons.'

Her mother's grey eyes darkened. 'Today, my whereupon thoughts are that he deserved to fall a cropper, after all, he did kick Rufus more than once when he thought I wasn't looking, and no rain in the world could hide that from me.'

'I know, I know a lot of things need not to be repeated.' A small secret smile began to lift the corners of Della's mouth and her eyes had a secluded look – a shut out look.

Her mother eyed the look with a drawn face as though she was sitting in church unable to understand, let alone lip-read the preacher's spoken words. 'You know what, my girl?' she asked in that certain tone only their children recognise.

Della brushed the crumbs from her lips with pity. 'We were, Mother, like bees starved of royal jelly seeking nourishment and we both agreed that Arthur was our obvious choice, remember?'

The old woman acknowledged the agreement only with eyelids.

Her daughter placed a knickerbocker glory dessert in front of her parent. 'This should sweeten you up, Mummy. Remember how you often fantasised about tasting such delights?'

Her mother ogled the tempting treat served in a tall, elegant crystal glass. 'I'll say just once, Della Ware, you're a common little cat whose fallen on her feet. This tempting sweetener looks like a sin dressed in its Sunday best.' She eyed it greedily. 'And it does have the look of something to do with providence.' She smiled awkwardly. 'Should I feel guilty if I had to eat it and enjoy it, considering Arthur is laid post position on a private hospital bed nursing his pains?'

'Not you,' Della said with affection if not admiration. 'Arthur said this morning with your forceful character you could be well able to keep an eye to the haulage business while he mends...'

Her mother stopped short of delivering a brim-full of dessert to her mouth in sheer astonishment. 'What!' She paid alert attention to her daughter. 'Are you telling me when you visited him this morning he was sat up in bed...' She was easily alerted.

'Eating a soft-bellied egg.'

'Soft-bellied egg! That would hardly be sufficient if he's already convalescing.' She swallowed the spoonful of delight not tasting the richness of flavours. 'Well, I'll be damned,' she said with sinuous grace. 'What I really want to know is Arthur still opposed to Rufus staying here as part of the family?'

'It's vital to stay patient, Mother. Arthur has already invited you and he'll not be ready to un-invite you or...' she hesitated, knowing it was a sensitive area.

The old woman who had endured poverty and pain now rather feared this open-endedness of the home arrangement. 'Patience,' she latched onto the provoking word. 'I feel thoroughly depleted by the turn of events. I need a leg-up. Is psychiatric counselling part of the release from the Evergreen care home?'

Della laughed unnecessarily loud. 'As a matter of fact, Arthur did say only this morning – if you could put your hand to carrying a watering can and a disposable bag every time you took the dog for exercise on the lawns while avoiding the maze, to flush and collect, then he could just about tolerate the situation and possibly sort out the difference.'

The old woman shivered with satisfaction. Suddenly, surprisingly, she felt well disposed towards him. 'I think I should get to know Arthur better.' She ladled out a further helping of the dessert and spooned it into her mouth before saying – thoughtfully, 'Yes, I think I should... I'd like to.' All at once, she looked 10 years younger. 'Which reminds me, while I was housed in that private people's home, a blue-stocking widow told me of a very old fashioned practice the gentry used to train a wayward canine to accept a new master.' Her smile was beguiling. It had an impact.

'Tell me, Mummy. Do tell.' Her daughter leaned eagerly over the hostess trolley. Even Della's heightened imagination could not imagine what the remedy offered. She squirmed uncomfortably enjoying the sensation.

'I'll tell you later, my girl.' Her mother was frugally scraping the last fruity bits of full rich flavours from the bottom of the crystal glass... but later the moment had passed.

WOULD YOU BELIEVE IT?

This story was first published in She And The Cat's Mother Monthly Recollections eMagazine (issue number 9) August 2022 via patreon.com/sheandthecatsmother

A neighbour, while browsing in Marks and Spencer overheard a woman saying to her companion:

"Oh, yes. My husband is still a loan manager at the Halifax bank, and the other day he was interviewing a woman who wanted a loan to pay for her divorce.

"David explained that loans were usually granted for household appliances or home improvements. Not batting an eyelid, earnestly she told him that a divorce WOULD be a home improvement."

THE TRADE OFF

To look at The Honourable Mrs Cyril Fredrick Johnson, shopping in the Co-op, Tesco, or Aldi supermarkets; she could not look less like her hereditary rank that most people imagined.

She was now dressed down, due to shame and blame caused by her rogue husband, Sir Cyril Fredrick Johnson, who passed away – voluntarily – leaving the family estate in dire debt; hence, the bank seized the big house and acreage, leaving her a "grace and favour" home; the Gate-Keeper's cottage which was sorely in need of modernisation, and; added to this down-grading, The Coterie – the privileged friends, had stopped including her within their frequent social meetings, leaving her feeling bruised and disconnected...

At that time, borne out of sheer frustration, a chance occurrence happened. It was not as though she had planned it. The happening was while she was at the self-service check-out feeling agitated as a result of a piece of lovely hand-cured pork refused to scan, despite several attempts to register.

The Lady, looked about herself for staff assistance for support – seeing no ready assistant available, and unable to sort the problem out herself – whatever it was that came over her she would never know, because never once in all her life had it ever crossed her mind to steal; not even a mint sweet from the open pick-n-mix displays.

Swallowing her irritation, she thought, if the proprietary named – preferred to save money to bolster their profits by installing machines rather than paying for extra human cashiers and helpers, then, just this once, I will – break free from the godly Methodist teachings, and, why not help myself by slipping the delicious looking pork (that induces salivation) into my shopping bag with the rest of the paid provisions?

So, feeling like herself, only different, The Hon. Mrs Cyril Fredrick Johnson's careful eyes wandered into vagueness as she sauntered towards the exit door – thinking: Don't go with the wind, dear Lady; it could blow you anywhere – which sent a shiver of anticipation of being caught red-handed. Yet, in spite of that expectation, enjoying – for the first time, the sensation of becoming invisible after the disgrace of her grandeur husband of 42-years, and, finding out who her real friends were...

Such cold comfort. Thus, she had discovered self-effacing armoury – not wanting to draw attention to herself – since she felt it, named it; the intensity of living on the line of genteel poverty, adaptability was the key. Her Ladyship feigned absent mindedness and casually left the building – unnoticed – a free woman.

:

It was only when the Lady returned to her shabby home, and plated the moreish pork sandwiches that she reflected upon her first ever risk-taking steal, and again the sudden source of pleasure cruised through her body, knowing she had secretly no intentions of returning the succulent wedge of pork.

'The pleasure is all mine,' she assured herself, and pleasure had been scarce throughout the testing years of her marriage and those later months. Furthermore, she knew the thrill of not being caught would never leave her. She hugged herself, then laughed brazenly. 'Oh, yes,' she the gentry, but cash-strapped member of the landed gentry had found her forte. The perfect antidote to counteract the humiliating circumstances outside her control. Bankruptcy! And, rejection!

Later on the Lady seated herself closer to the grate fire; then poured out a full glass of her favourite wine, with a smile of expectancy. It did not disappoint; which brought her mind strictly back to her married children; both residing in distant communities, conveniently tallied with their absence since the big house and land had been sold-off – their heritage – causing a preferment of family chaos, leaving her feeling sick, tired, and the mirror reflected back to her – oh yes, she looked as bad as she felt. These dire consequences were taking their toll on her. Poverty did not become her.

The turning point, she acknowledged some months later, had been triggered when she was out shopping within the most expensively priced supermarket, and the lovely piece of pork refused to be scanned. The Honourable Mrs Cyril Fredrick Johnson, sipped graciously, the self-chosen brand of wine – marvelling at the way it tasted so much more deliciously when stolen – had she really been frustrated or had she been tempted to make that first ever steal?

She consoled herself by placing another coal dust briquette upon the smouldering fire. She leaned back on the chair. Should she confess to her children? Would they understand, stealing this and that was the only thing that made her able to abide degrading circumstances? Would they ever know the thrill, the adrenalin that pumps through one's body when one gets away with it? Perhaps not. Gone from plain sight, the woman who was admired, even envied for being the most assiduous committee member of the Women's

Rights Division, now portraying herself as a nonentity – galling – but a necessity. Now she was someone like her other, but different.

The Honourable Mrs Cyril Fredrick Johnson was no longer disturbed about herself. She was very nearly without self-pity.

STRATEGY

This story was first published in She And The Cat's Mother Monthly Recollections eMagazine (issue number 2) December 2021 via patreon.com/sheandthecatsmother

The story goes something like this:

Hill-farmer, Jacob Wilcox, a confirmed bachelor, well known for his evasive skill of avoiding marriage; as usual, attended the spring sheep sales, held on the outskirts of his local market town, where he came unexpectedly upon a past courtship – a shepherdess, an attentive woman, whom he had not seen for many years. On impulse, he sanely invited her back to his remote farm for supper.

She, knowing from yesterdays relationship, he was too selfish to share himself; and knowing it's hope that kills; recklessly accepted his invitation.

Later, when they were tucking into the fish and chips supper, she noticed – often – his border collie was sagaciously watching every mouthful of food she ate. Feeling inquisitive she enquired, "Why is your dog setting me?"

"Oh, don't bother yourself about old lassie," he said. "You're eating off her plate."

BLESSING IN DISGUISE

It was an unexpected glorious sunny morning of late September day when Gilbert Heseltine, ex-Country Sprint Champion, stood perfectly still, gazing with hungry eyes into the forget-me-not blue sky; seeing while hearing thousands of migrant swallows in flight, soaring, trilling and swirling in unison while tweeting clearly their farewell songs before beginning their journey back to their homeland – unknowingly – awakening the dull ache of his own yearning to recapture the loss of a renowned foot-race career. It had been the only thing in his life that he had really cared about – nurtured to the point of obsession – and the loss of it was like an absence constantly attending to his misery and longing...

A renewed chill of remorse shivered down his back. After all, he reckoned, he had been celebrated as a trailblazer. The potato couches favourite bet, until he was plagued with ligament problems which cancelled out his velvety tread. Gilbert's eyes glazed over with saltwater; blurring sky-blue and forktails into shadows of inseparable companions.

'It's hard to see the back of something you love,' he muttered, lowering his eyes. It was at that divide of a moment, he decided to plan a comeback. 'If those tiny fragile birds can travel thousands of miles every year, over the English Channel, across France, through Spain, across the Mediterranean sea, over the Atlas mountains and jungle to Africa their homeland.' Gilbert's lips outlined a shadowy smile. Why not a comeback? He reasoned. A 20-mile practice sprint was of little moment. Once more he looked up into the sky, lost in composition... 'Could these tiny resilient birds – by nature – have inborn knowledge to magnetic entrances of time-space corridors, thus saving them thousands of turbulent miles of travel?' Gilbert had to sit down before he fell down.

Gilbert cursed like a trouper under his breath. Nobody wanted him much after he had retired from the sporting arena, or even cared much whether he was present or not; so cricket groundwork – at weekends, became the recipient of the distress no-one wished to pay attention to.

Gilbert's grey eyes darkened with discontentment. Even his meritorious mowing, raking, clearing-up and the business of composting waste; likewise, pre-rubbing the cricket balls against the inside of his thighs like the professional players. Jobbing! Jobs taken for granted.

Another expletive escaped from between his

compressed lips. He was certain in his own certainty, if he'd been caught urinating over the balls instead – anyone – if caring enough, would have found him alive, if not precisely well. With a singleness of attention, Gilbert pushed his fly-buttons through their buttonholes – thinking... '10 years ago I was a forefront hero, now I'm a forgotten nobody... in my heyday, if I'd been caught sprinting up someone's driveway, I would have been recognised and invited indoors for a drink and a bite too eat...' Gilbert continued to talk to himself – about himself – he didn't know any better.

:

Before Gilbert went off the boil, he discussed his comeback plan with colleagues while restoring brown furniture in the chilly dank backroom within an old building erected in the shadow of a water-tower. It was rented property – the renter – not a particularly grateful employer, kept them overworked and underpaid.

They, his colleagues, had with good intentions, reminded him that his glory days were long gone, and his youth had passed into middle-aged. So, as an alternative, perhaps he should consider putting his bachelor days at rest and find himself an honest, reliable, childbearing woman to set his restless mind at peace...

Gilbert never asked for their advice again. He distanced himself from their indifferences. Later, he returned to the single room where he slept, kept his clothes and solitary belongings, but hardly spent time eating there. He preferred snacking from near-by snack-bars, and fish and chip takeaways. He had no interest in domesticity. He, a confirmed bachelor of the bohemian kind – although he did make an occasional appearance with an occasional female – he had gained the reputation of having that rare skill of evading matrimony, selfish by being the alfresco type of person. Gilbert did not want to even consider such questioning. He was a loner.

His regular work colleagues bantered their differences towards his belated comeback, spoken loud enough for him to pretend not to hear. Nevertheless, he rose above their raillery by having the last word.

'The way I see my attempts to regain a welcoming comeback is quite plain to me if not to yourselves,' he'd reasoned with barbed unreasoning. 'I don't want to spend the rest of my working years polishitting brown furniture.' Afterwards, he could not remember making such an unsanitary remark.

:

Feeling a leak of happiness by the prospect of himself taking the decision to control his comeback, Gilbert eagerly entered the single room where he resided. Closing the door firmly behind him before making a bee-line for the cardboard box beneath his camp-bed, wherein, thick layers of yellowing media pages and cut-outs covering his successful sprinting career and beneath them his personal note-worthy diary. A diary where he'd fastidiously entered all his yearly routes, mileage, times, places, roads, junctions, weather conditions, diet table and health tips, even down to his physiologist's name and telephone numbers – an A4 carrier bag, holding all the information he needed. 'That's all there is...' he enunciated from the foot of the bed. 'But it's plenty.'

Energised, Gilbert threw himself down onto the portable bed and began to cycle his legs in the air as he contemplated his past career. He closed his feasting eyes to let his mind's eye indulge in the raving reviews and the smiling, laughing images of himself – so blond, tanned, yet prone to amorous distractions. A maverick; standing proudly on the winners' podiums. He hugged his knees to his chest. Yes. He had been so very happy then, but afraid to share his happiness in case it vanished. Gilbert opened his eyes only to see flaking paint curling on the ceiling. He squirmed unintentionally as mind over matter began to prowl into his past disabilities – all kicking in, one by one, like uninvited cold-callers. Cramps, torn muscles and sprains. It had been pride and self-preservation that had mercilessly drove him onto finishing the final seasonal sprinting games; knowing he was all hell-bent on winning the golden title: The Country Sprint Champion.

The set-back had happened when he was approximately half-way from the finishing post when he'd experienced a sudden spasmodic contraction within the muscle of his left leg which had almost put paid to his famous velvety tread. He remembered glancing over his shoulder to see if any other sprinter was in sight. No-one! Relieved beyond measure, he'd looked ahead of himself, just in time to see two male stewards disappear into a portable toilet erected near to the crossroads. How he'd sprinted with such debilitating pain... God only knew! All he chose to recall was that he'd manually swivelled the route signpost, with its indicating fingerpost, to point in the opposite direction. This diversion, he'd known, would add an extra 6 miles to the organised route before other road-signs pointed them onto the original foot-race course, so mercifully, gaining him recovery time and with Lady Luck attending his commonality, he would be celebrated as The

Country Sprint Champion. Something to get exercised about. 'Does anyone ever know when they do something for the last time..?' The answer did not allow elegant inner reflection.

Untimely alerted from his memories, Gilbert became aware that the evening had already drawn in and the room had cooled. The only warmth came from the pencil slim glow from the pilot flame of the gas boiler flickering blue and yellow in his draught of rising from his bed with renewed buoyancy. 'I still feel young... if no longer young...' he heard himself talking to himself. 'Why, it was only last weekend when I celebrated my fortieth birthday with a can of beer and a pork-pie while admiring the late summer blooms in the Valley Gardens; blooms still smelling of sunshine – quite unlike me.'

Gilbert gritted his teeth. He didn't need anyone to tell him that he'd lost sight of his old self – the hero – the notoriety, the recognition; applause, admiration, warmth, even envy – instead, he got indifference – a fore-goner, lost for the last 10 years of endlessly French polishing inanimate objects which had seriously modified his personality. He'd forgotten how to be happy. 'Time to move on...' he muttered. 'I want memories that can give you a wonderful tailwind.'

Without deflecting from his mission, Gilbert started methodically to clear a space in the shadows of the far corner of the workplace, where a window the size of an air-vent let in a shaft of daylight depicting his makeshift apparatus, adapted, with heightened imagination. There was no stopping him now. With bountiful energy, Gilbert began his training. It was manic! His fitness programme started by him laying on his back on the flagged stone floor, toes hooked round a work-bench foot-bar which enabled him to rise then lean backwards, press-ups, skipping over and under a cart-rope. Raising dumb-bells filled with clay soil, iron implements held aloft on the spot – all 50 times – consequentially, he broke out in hot then cold flushes, dizziness, nausea, cramps and worrying palpitations which left him feeling as though he'd been climbing Mount Everest without any safety.

Eventually, he realised his work colleagues could see more than they could stand to see. Evidently through the red mist of intemperance, Gilbert cottoned onto the plain fact they were as unsettled as he was. This unsettlement made him able to bear their constant observations during their half-hour tea-break, and to add insult to injury, he knew they were paying inordinate attention to his most sensitive area – the hard round stomach that rested over his belt.

They spoke, as he now expected, loud enough for him to feign not to hear – he counting out his numbers loudly... '24... 25... 26...'

One said, 'You'd think a grown man would have more sense. If he's not careful, he'll be all washed out before he'll even know it.'

The other said, 'Does he not know that he's slipped from youth to middle age. All this excessive exercise could result in a cardiac arrest and–'

Another said, 'Do we know anything about resuscitation?'

The fourth one replied, 'Well, I've kissed a few pettifoggery guys in my time, but Gilbert...' he pulled silly faces and stuck out his tongue then wriggled it around his lips. 'Nah, why tempt a relationship.'

They laughed, enjoying the assumption of friendly banter.

'I don't think the old boy has found his feet again,' said the first speaker. 'I mean, it's not as though he has any sort of home-life to take his mind off this obsession of recapturing the spotlight.'

The other one had to be heard, 'As far as I know he has no living relations to speak of and no partner on the horizon–'

'And now we're seeing the belligerent side to his nature,' interrupted another. 'I wouldn't be surprised if he'd quarrelled with them all and they in turn had cut him out of their wills. Now, that would explain why he's living in a one room flat.'

'A quarter house pertaining to neighbourhood gossip,' offered the fourth one. 'Apparently they are quite the rage these days for low-earners and single people and...'

Their voices faded as they distanced themselves to take the 10 a.m. tea-break, leaving Gilbert feeling as though he'd acquired an attack of migraine through eating blue stilton cheese. He needed no-one to tell him that he'd been in limbo for 9 years, doing much jobbing jobs to duck memories of early retirement due to his injuries, which still left a dull ache of loss. Instead of retaliating verbally, he would reach out for a stick of celery or rhubarb and crunch and crush it between his teeth – perfect teeth – while poised, elbows pointing outwards... one hand on one hip while continuing his high jinks.

'By jingo,' said the fourth one, closing his eyes in ecstasy of mind. 'He's a sadist.'

'Steady on now,' rebuffed the other one who had a sporting streak in his nature. 'I know you get tense when you're excited, but give the ex-champ a bit of credit and respect, Gilbert still holds the record of having sprinted in the shortest recorded time...'

Heads slowly turned to squint into the shadows of the far corner of the work-room to pin-point the light and shade figure of the retiree still rising and lowering himself with the aid of the bench-bar.

'I can still picture him sprinting along so effortlessly–' the other was beginning to warm to his recall. 'The press constantly referred to his velvet tread.' A smile actually sounded in his voice – not lost – causing quizzical eyebrows to arch and mouths to tighten, but he'd started and was going to finish. 'I was actually there when Gilbert completed his last triumphant foot-race wherein, he accomplished a new record breaking time, and he still looked invigorated when stepping proudly onto the winners' podium to receive the gold meddle from a royal member – and... while the crowds were still applauding – he shockingly announced his retirement–'

'Did he give an explanation?' interrupted the first one impatiently, 'and how did he look and sound when he made the announcement?'

'Preoccupied,' came the immediate response. 'But later when interviewed by the BBC about his ligament and cramp problems, he said that he'd little appetite for comfort or the luxury of moods as he'd always elevated himself above pain-barriers which had always caused misery and joy.'

'Pain and pleasure,' the second one mused, taking a deep bite out of his square of moist parkin, 'such toeholds.' He tongued aside the wedge of cake. 'Gilbert should have been kept well away from the glare of television.'

Gilbert, easily alerted, despite grunting in the throes of lifting clay-filled dumb-bells aloft, could hear in their voices discontentment... 'I am a reproach to them,' he enunciated, 'but a necessity.' He smiled. Just. Hearing the scraping of chair legs against the stone floor as they vacated their seats to go and finish off the morning tea-break with a cigarette or a visit to the outside latrines, and as their talking for talking sake faded into the out-distance, he balked, thinking: They're like pouting pigeons – if only they knew.

In love he had been and still was underprivileged. He could never forgive his indifferent parents for withholding their time and affection from him. So bloody selfish and righteous, believing children should be seen but not heard. He rocked from his heel to toe as he thrust the dumb-bells to the rafters; then clearing his throat, all done with the patience of Jobe, which he recognised as scheming... perhaps evil... 'Nah,' he was on a personal mission. '48... 49... 50...'

:

Autumn passed through into winter with noticeable changes. Gilbert was by now, very nearly a vegetarian and his body was beginning to show positive results – they noticed – such pin-pointing moments were Gilbert's rewards. He was no longer disturbed by their back-biting and their constant habit of talking all over his words thus making conversation not worth the effort. So, with the skill of long practice, Gilbert moonlighted his training gear above the workplace, likewise his refrigerator, he stored fresh vegetables, fresh fruits, nuts, herbs, juices, dried apricots, raisins, sultanas and packets of vitabiotic supplements. He was on a rollercoaster. Even a blind man would have seen that...

Come May, Gilbert had lost 4 stone in weight and gained a visible 6-pack, and furthermore – they noted – he looked 10 years younger, more like his old self, more like a champion in his heyday.

The consensus of his work colleagues to their knowledge, he'd never had a useful lover to dampen down his bachelor days or his oddity. One said, what they'd all been thinking, 'If his art of gymnastics was anything to go by, he'd be too dangerous to love.'

May day, the day Gilbert had deliberately inked into his daily diary as the special day for his first trial performance, a 10 mile sprint route. A modified try-able distance from his past malleable 20 mile courses. He felt so happy – dared not to show it in case it forsaked him.

The night before he'd hardly slept. His mind had been far too occupied tracing and retracting every inch of his chosen route with a dogged patience that often won. Throwing aside his bedclothes he took himself outside to shower in the backyard beneath a hosepipe attached to the cold water tap.

Invigorated, returning back to his room to stand in front of the mirror assessing himself in the measured way that men and women do when their bodies are commodities... seeing himself being reflected as a person of interest – seeing himself very nearly as he use to look; blond, tousled hair now showing signs of turning silver-grey. A man of intuition and instinct... a man who followed his own mind-set over matter. His interested grey eyes darkened, he'd come too far to be distracted by anyone or anything. He saluted his reflection, then smiled – but the smile did not reach his bold eyes. Could they, the unconvertibles have cottoned onto the fact that their blatant bantering had been like bitter peppers spicing up the gruelling training? Himself knowing, he'd have to do some fast and hard work to plug the 9 year gap. Gilbert squared his shoulders. He felt remarkably strong, and in an odd way – wonderful.

10 minutes to 10 a.m. found Gilbert already dressed in his former sport's gear, standing only a stone throw from his starting place, the water tower. The early morning mist had cleared giving him a clear view of the landscape and high-rise buildings that scraped the Bank Holiday blue sky. It was going to be a fine day. A day to relish the smell of warmed tarmac beneath the soles of his trainers.

Gilbert rechecked his wristwatch. 8 minutes to 10 a.m. To kill time he began to rhythmically rock from toes to heels while rechecking his penned route and memorandum outlined in red link... he spoke aloud to bring them breath, 'No headmost sprinting. No unequal rhythm at curbs and junctions – and not to be waylaid by a foot-passenger wanting directions.'

He rechecked his watch. 6 minutes to 10 a.m. Still time to adjust the strap on his across-body bag holding a bottle of mineral water and a handful of barley sweets. 'Nah!' Stopping, even pausing had never been on his agenda. Dehydration and fatigue, he knew from experience, did not photograph well.

Gilbert rechecked his watch. 4 minutes to 10 a.m.

Acquainted with waiting, Gilbert took time to remove his sunglasses from his back pocket to breath over the shades before polishing them thoroughly with the hem of his sport's shirt. Defected vision was not an option. There was always the possibility of bumping into cyclists, dog walkers failing responsibilities for their pets' actions, crocodile queues of school-leaving children awaiting to crossover a busy road. All with unforeseen hap-hazards enough to rob any competitive athlete of precious seconds, even minutes. Gilbert unwrapped a barley sugared sweet and crunched it into jagged pieces, thinking: Nothing, simply nothing will impinge upon my comeback.

Gilbert rechecked his watch. 2 minutes to 10 a.m. 'Hardly able to rein-in his excitement, he headed for the neighbouring bridle path aligned to the water tower premise to confirm if the wooden peg he had inserted into the ground earlier was still there. It was exactly as he'd left it with a lick of mahogany polish on its head. He tilted a smile and glanced up towards the wide sky, feeling the breaths of wind wafting the sweet, tangible aromas of spring – an attendance entirely captivating to anyone who was prepared to be captivated – and Gilbert was as ready as a new moon at spring-tide.

The ex-champion rechecked his watch. 1 minute to 10 a.m. He smiled distantly as he cast a quick glance towards the warehouse, wherein his work colleagues, he knew, would be seated already for their 10 a.m. tea-break and cold cut sandwiches. Had they a notion of his whereabouts? 'Nah!' They had been paying him small attention, particularly since he had removed himself and his equipment to the upper-room – and yes, if he had heard one, if not more of them, shouting from the bottom of the stairs, or the foot of the landing that he was stirring up dust from his manic activities and it was bloody well floating down between the floor-broads onto everyone and everything...

Gilbert was in no position to argue. To settle the differences, he'd confiscated a roll of second-hand carpet from the adjoining sale-rooms: that could have been construed as having been charity over-kill, but necessary... the only sane thing to do under the circumstances.

Gilbert rechecked his watch. 10 seconds to 10 a.m. He laughed raucously and gestured out of all proportions towards the warehouse, shouting, 'Bon-nots! Bon-nots!' as incoherently as he dared... He couldn't stop, nor did he want to until the Town Hall clock chimes resounded off the water tower. On a wave of euphoria, Gilbert sprinted over the imaginary starting line with the agility of his former days. He felt great. The morning sun was warm on his back, gentle enough to be kind to his emotions, awakening a sense of peace and freedom as he sprinted along the bridle path; seeing sheep grazing leisurely on the pasture land with their spring lambs frolicking about them in the growing grasses and wild flowers. Such a pleasant pleasure, thought Gilbert – such a contrast from the argy-bargy of questionable remarks within the workplace. Particularly when he didn't want to even reconsider such raw questioning after realising he'd embodied his ideal plan of a comeback into words. There was no going back. He'd come too far.

Gilbert glanced at his watch. He was well within his calculated time as he reached the far closed gate, knowing he would have sprinted the first mile of his 10 mile route. Closing the farm gate behind himself, Gilbert turned right, as planned, and proceeded to sprint towards the hamlet of Penthwaite, passed the grocer's shop wherein, the local post office operated, passed the cricket ground and the bowling green; aware of the muffled voice and the clicking of a ball against the bat accompanied by the dull sound of intermittent clapping; all striking the known chords in his memory. He passed the stone built houses with their grey slate roofs. He smiled, remembering also that in his heyday, he would have been invited indoors for dinner or tea. His jaw tightened. Now they would say – 'Who?'

With renewed fire in his belly, Gilbert sprinted his way down the steep slope of a hill to where it gradually levelled out towards crossroads. No sooner had his feet touched the gravel direction, he rechecked his time schedule – so deep was his concentration upon his sacred timetable, for some reason or another, instead of turning right, he turned left, not realising until he raised his eyes from the road to become aware of the unfamiliar tree-lined avenue road with a grass verge wherein, harebells, scarlet pimpernels and sweet violets spearheaded through green uncut grasses – not quite country, and not quite town. Instinctively, he raised his eyesight to take in the substantial private properties with ornate chimney-pots custom-built for people who had made their money in the last war but who had tried to keepsake the fact for the last 40 years.

Gilbert's lips curled downwards in an expression of obstinacy which masked his ruthlessness. 'Don't look back,' he told himself. 'That would be like accidentally putting one's sport shirt on the wrong side out... consequence... the unlooked-for incident.' He paused in mid-stride, recalling the dilemma of driving his father's brand-new car into the local supermarket indoor carpark at a jaunty angle and the lift doors closed on the vehicle when he was barely half-way through them, and the automatically programmed doors proceeded to go forwards and backwards – forwards and backwards until the car was crushed with himself still strap-belted in the driver's seat, even worse, his comfortably-off father had never let him forget. The consequence, he'd never drove a vehicle again. In place of that chilling experience, he'd taken to sprinting.

Gathering his bearings, Gilbert began to sprint on the spot while unwrapping a barley sweet, then rechecked his watch whilst surveying the unfamiliar neighbourhood into which he had unintentionally brought himself. It was while he was speculating, he became aware of a woman walking on the pavement. She was carrying in each hand a tote bag full of merchandise. Her hair, he noted sagely, was held back by sunglasses perched on her head, and furthermore she was quite plump in a fetching way, though she had an eye-catching swing with her hips emphasised by the flared frock that grazed the back of her bare tanned legs and on her feet she wore sandals. She looked rationally homely, and approachable. Perhaps... perhaps – he thought sanely, he could catch-up to her to enquire if there was a short-cut to his last post, The Blue Bovine Public House?

Gilbert rechecked his watch. Yes, still in-time schedule. He hesitated. Should he back-away or man-up? Women! He'd never had a grateful lover. He could still feel the backlash of the last woman he'd bedded down. Gilbert tried to blink the preposterous image of her sipping a double vodka through a bent straw with ice cubes tinkling throughout the unsatisfactory on and off coupling which had ended in chastening chaos.

He squared his shoulders and began to hum the National Anthem while casting sagacious side-glances up and down the avenue; detecting a lace curtain beginning to tweak and an open window reflecting movement. 'Move on – keep moving on...' his inner voice commanded, 'before you get accused of stalking.'

Without losing another precious second, Gilbert re-gathered himself together. He was good at that. Use to that. With the skill of practice he closed the road gap between them, to halt alongside her, instantly seeing she was a bonnie woman with rosy complexion, fine dark eyes, hair to match, rose-bud lips and pretty teeth.

'Excuse me, dear lady.' He smiled persuasively, hoping she could be persuaded, 'but I've lost my way. Am I on the right track for, The Blue Bovine Public House? If so, I've a few minutes to spare, and I could not help noticing that you look weighed down with shopping, so, in exchange for your given directions, may I lend you a helping hand?' Gilbert said all this without pausing for breath. He'd never, ever, encroached so boldly into a woman's space or time before – what came over him, he would never know.

She allowed the request to hang in the air without embarrassment. Then she said, 'What a noble gesture...' her pink lips creased into a smile, 'considering that I don't have far to go.'

He, not wanting to lose a moment of recognition said sagely, 'I'd like to introduce myself.' He held out his hand while automatically rocking backwards and forwards on his feet. 'I use to be a professional sprinter so I can recognise a tiresome gait a mile off...' He tilted an engaging smile – knowing it always use to photograph so well, 'so if help is offered with good will, it should be taken, not wasted.'

Acting on her own judgement, she turned to face him squarely... thinking: The public eye can see a villain where only a minute before he was a hero...

She eyed his tousled blond hair, his rustic complexion, his lean, mean body and suddenly became exquisitely aware of herself. 'I shall take advantage of your kind offer,' she mirrored his smile and handed one of her hessian bags to him, while saying, 'I don't make a practice of handing over provisions, but just this once.'

They walked side by side for several yards before coming to a row of iron railings guarding the frontage of a row of three-storey period houses with four steps leading to their front doors. With a deep sigh of relief she paused at the second step to place the other copious bag beside her, then slowly began to unstrap her sandals.

Gilbert hovered momentarily before deciding to place an arm along the railing spikes, still gripping the other tote bag with his other hand. He could not take his eyes off her – heard her groan with pleasure as she wriggled and flexed her toes seductively in the gentle breeze.

'I should have known not to have bought plastic footwear,' she grimaced. 'They're so unfriendly and blistering.' The foot-sore woman crossed one shapely leg over the other, giving Gilbert a glimpse of satin lace. 'Leather...' her rosy expression spelt out her meaning before she explained – 'Leather does allow one's body to breath.'

Gilbert didn't answer. He was too lost in the look on her face.

She caught his eye. 'By the way, I'm Maggie,' not waiting for his reply, she dipped into the tote bag, moving things about before producing a handful of early green beans, whereupon, she podded and tailed each one, in turn, before popping them into her mouth.

From the foot of the steps, Gilbert's eyes detected a smile of intention. He moved himself with sinuous grace onto the bottom step. 'Call me Bert.' His laugh was unnecessary. 'Brevity for Gilbert.'

'I've heard about you, although I don't recognise you, but then, I'm not a sport's enthusiast,' she spoke through a full mouth of broad beans, 'but I've always admired the grace of athletes.'

Gilbert had never pretended to understand women. He twisted his neck sideways to look at the woman seated on the step above him; sensing the scent of promise. It sweetened him... encouraged him.

Eyes bright with purpose, Maggie lowered her sight to take in the look of interest from interested eyes, then shrewdly, veiled her eyes to nimbly thumb a row of pulses off their seed-bed. They fell like a row of dominoes onto the palm of her hand. Smiling she outstretched her hand to him. 'For you, Bert. Try them. They're as sweet as a nut.'

Amused with the offering, he cupped his hand in readiness. 'They look as right as rain,' he said. He'd had a plain breakfast. How long they sat there shelling, eating and talking like old acquaintances, he had no inkling. They'd captured the mood of the spring morning without him once rechecking his watch. It wasn't until Maggie began to scoop the empty shells of the beans from the droop of her dress between her thighs that he became aware of the passing of time – to find himself pleasantly surprised – 'Maggie,' he sounded normal to his own ears, 'I never expected more than a mild hello and a cool goodbye.'

'Touché,' she laughed crushing the paper bag now holding the vegetable empty pods into an untidy shape. 'What I really fancy right now is a lovely cup of tea.' She rose while holding onto her shopping and handbag.

Gilbert bounded up the steps. 'I'll gladly brew you a pot of tea, just direct me to the kitchen.' He opened the front door, turned to find her one step behind him.

'Just follow your nose, Bert,' she laughed. She was infectious and today, Gilbert was capable of being infected without thinking he was doing anything unusual.

The hallway, he noted shrewdly, was spacious and furnished with ornate furniture. An elderly man was seated on an easy chair obscurely under the alcove of a stairway. He held a glass half-filled with distilled spirit in one hand, and an unlit cigar between two fingers of the other hand.

'Oh, bless you,' he said to neither he or she. 'I've been waiting an age for the invited ones to arrive, and the paper boy hasn't shown up either.'

'Just be patient a little longer,' said Gilbert pleasantly, his words taking him down the adjacent corridor where the smell of cooking lingered.

'And don't forget the honey to sweeten my tea.' The old man raised his voice. It's beneficial towards my painful arthritis.' Catching Maggie's eyes added, 'and it keeps the bugs at bay.

Maggie lowered herself onto the chaise longue and slowly sank down against the flock cushions. 'I don't know much about arthritis, dear, but I do know that plastic plays havoc with one's feet, especially when the sun's out...' She crossed one leg over the knee of the other and began to dab each blister-bladder with her handkerchief while shushing and blowing breath upon them as though cooling hot soup.

Sooner than later, Gilbert appeared carrying a tray whereupon, a teapot, three cups and saucers, milk jug, sugar-pot and a jar of honey were arranged. He placed the tray on a side-table and proceeded to pour out a first cup of tea.

'I'll have the first pour out, if you don't mind,' said the old man, 'I like it weak with a splash of white water and a generous spoonful of organic honey.'

Gilbert obliged with efficacy and an intended portion of necessity.

The old man spoke in a state of reveries. 'I must stop looking at men as though they are women. It's sheer madness.'

'Madness,' repeated Gilbert ironically, 'can provide

people with religious comfort, and it tends to make civilisation appear attainable.'

'Marginally the better option,' Maggie looked uneasy, 'but always worth a second chance. 'She opened her handbag and began to rummage amongst its contents.

Quick to steal the frown from her brow, Gilbert lowered his gaze, thinking: It's crucial to stay in such a rare accidental occurrence – so I must not let it pass me by.

Without a second thought, Gilbert removed the side-table bearing the tea-tray and placed it before the chaise longue, then sat down beside her to pour out a second cup of tea. 'I always think the second cup of tea never tastes as good as the first one, Maggie.' He offered a quiet smile of expectancy...

She smiled back into his face. 'I'll have it as it comes, Bert. A hot drink, weak or strong does quench one's thirst better than cold tap water.'

Gilbert allowed exasperation to sound in his voice. 'These days I usually live on cold cut sandwiches and cold bottled beer and cream crackers. Convenience food. Easy preference food when living on my own with small attention.'

'Little things can sometimes mean a lot,' she murmured, stirring a spoonful of honey into her tea.

'I've had enough of small uncertainties, now I want certainties.'

Their eyes met and rested upon each other's outlook...

She thought: I can detect careful concentration, as though he's disposing of a depth charge... he's too dangerous to love...

He thought: Given the brevity of our acquaintance she does have kind eyes and they do sparkle from light to shade... she's just human sunshine. And the thought caressed his heart. 'Maggie,' Gilbert spoke loudly so he could hear his own voice above the throbbing pulse in his temples. 'I know we met accidentally due to myself taking an uncalculated turning during my trial run, but my mistake came by pure chance...' his voice wavered, 'an unexpected, unlooked for chance. Furthermore, I'm enjoying the best mid-morning break in my unsatisfactory mid-life crisis...'

'Crisis,' she said. 'Just for a moment I thought you was going to say mid-life virus.' She giggled as incoherently as she dared.

He laughed. 'You're as good as a tonic, Maggie.'

'Not toxic then, Bert?'

'No.' He paid pleasing attention to her face. 'Nobody deserves that toxicant. Another cup of tea, Maggie?'

At that precise moment of intimacy, the front door was flung open, and an angry man – followed by an equally angry woman. 'How many times do I have to keep telling you that to embody an assumption in words half-creates it.'

The man ran a forefinger under his shirt collar. 'I'm as innocent as the day is long–'

'That won't wash with me,' she shouted. 'I've heard that lame excuse a dozen times before and the slate has never been wiped completely clean.'

'As you well know,' he outstretched his arms. 'I'm incapable of producing a spare...' The man continued to shout. 'You suffer from delusions and jealously... and I certainly don't have memory on that score whatsoever, so I can swear to you, darling–'

'Don't you darling me, you rone. You're stretching loyalties beyond repair. You're a fallacious, unreliable little so and so.' She slammed the door shut, leaving herself close on his heels.

'I'd be grateful if you didn't show me up in front of strangers.' His eyes swept over Maggie and Gilbert then to the old man who were now sitting up-right on their seating. 'You're becoming tiresome with your accusations, besides, I doubt that I would or could be capable of forcing myself onto another woman even if I was paid.' He forced a laugh. 'As you well know, darling, my diminutive size needs cohesion – remember – the consulter diagnosed the nature of my predicament as something perilously close to hermaphrodite.'

'Her-maf-rod-it!' Gilbert enunciated, rising swiftly to his feet thinking an explanation could be lost in translation. Surely a diversion was required, 'I thought this was your house, Maggie?'

Maggie looked a little flustered, 'I thought this house was yours, Bert. I mean, the positive way you headed up the stairs and down to the kitchen...'

'Come on, let's get on with it,' muttered Gilbert, unconsciously slipping back into his Northern dialect. 'And let's make ourselves scarce.' He grabbed Maggie's sandals and provision bags and headed down the passageway as though he was in a foot-race.

'Seems like the proper solution,' gasped Maggie.

She seized her handbag and ran barefoot after him while carefully avoiding the hostile eyes of the angry couple still parading about for attention, while overhearing the old man calling, 'And close the door behind you. I don't want to be caught in a cross-draft or I'll end up between two brass handles.'

'I thought this was your house,' repeated Gilbert, poised uneasily at the bottom of the outside steps. 'You looked so at home when you rested on these steps podding beans.'

'And I thought this house was your home by the way you took charge to brew the tea, and the excellent way you attended to the old man's whims. I truly thought he was your father.' Maggie vacated the steps. She couldn't have put one foot in front of the other quicker, even without the inflated blisters. 'I've a divorce pending so I don't want to be sighted entering and departing a house of suspected ill repute–'

'And I don't want to be classed as a nobody who's leading a bohemian lifestyle,' he interrupted – he had to be heard out, 'as I said to you earlier, Maggie, I'm on a mission to re-establish myself in the sport's arena. I was The Country Sprint Champion, and if any misunderstanding gets out and into the Sunday newspapers the reporters' words will be like flies parading on a dung-heap.'

'In my experience, one should never put the receiver down on such experienced muck-rakers. We must keep one step ahead of them, Bert.' Her mouth tightened at the edges. 'Only the blessed can be ungrateful.' She fell into uneven steps alongside him. 'We're only a stone throw from where I live, so if you care to drop off my provisions we could...' she smiled right into his heart, 'take the shortcut through the park to the Blue Bovine Public House for a refreshing beverage and the warm embrace of a chair.'

Gilbert had never had such engaging winning of words with a woman before. He lowered his head to get a better look at her face, she raised her head a little to help. A tender moment attended them; liken to the tide coming in quietly, making sounds of sentences without words.

Gilbert coughed to show breeding. 'I've always lived by propitiation and reputation and–' Suddenly his reverie was broken by a flashback; could he confess to Maggie what he could hardly admit to himself: How he'd won the title of The Country Sprint Champion...? No... He would take this secret to his grave. He cleared his throat... His eyes watered. 'It's the damn pollen,' he croaked, while mentally crossing his chest. Now the lie had to be permanent. A keepsake. The very thought of him being stripped of the title and gold medal threatened him to break-out in a profuse lather. Gilbert coughed again to give embellishment upon any otherwise trail of thoughts. His eyes re-watered.

'Poor you,' Maggie said mercifully, dabbing compassionately upon his over-flow of saltwater with her soiled handkerchief. 'It's the fecundating dust. It gets everywhere this time of year,' she laughed companionably. 'Pollen is the male element of flowers.'

Sustained by the unknown, Gilbert rashly said,

'Opportunities must be seized Maggie-May. Since turning middle-aged they haven't come too often my way. Our meeting was an accident without embarrassment. I feel as though I've known you forever.'

She, a woman of substance met his bold stare without a trace of self-consciousness. She linked her arm through his. 'Everyone is someone born for another, Bert, and sometimes the results can be spectacular.'

CIVILITY

This story was first published in She And The Cat's Mother Monthly Recollections eMagazine (issue number 8) June 2022 via patreon.com/sheandthecatsmother

A single pensioner and her Scotch Terrier dog, by way of shelter from the rain, headed into Waterstones, unaware of a Book Signing Event.

The purse-strapped pensioner didn't buy a book, and her Terrier dog could not read – but an audience of two is an audience and will exaggerate in numbers by word of mouth...

"How many attended?"

"Oh, just two... err... dozen or more..."

"A companionable gathering..."

"One woman brought her dog!"

THE SHARP ELBOW

This story was first published in She And The Cat's Mother newsletter/email via BrazenBitch.com (July 2024)

It was precisely 3:11 a.m. on a chilly morning when she woke abruptly from a deep sleep.

He did not. Snoring did not affect him.

It did her. She directed a sharp elbow to his ribs.

He snorted some more – rolled over – taking the lion's share of the duvet...

She, at the mercy of her emotions, decided life was too short.

She had to find an outlet; free herself from feeling like "brome" the weed that competes with barley for nutrients and sunshine.

4:13 a.m. Still awake – planning, how to stop marginal thinking?

After all, the children had left home some time ago; a reminded, one could not overstate the untidiness of human nature.

Her eyes rested on the vague outline ensconced within the duvet, wherein – yet again – a crescendo of sounds scalded her mind.

She continued to lay prostrate – ankles crossed – with the attitude of pained attention to the quality of their lifestyle.

All they had to live on now, was his pension; no longer a generous bounty from a not particularly grateful country.

A flicker of irritation played around her mouth.

Their married life had lost much of what others had gained.

They'd been seldom together except for hurried meals and intermittent nights, wherein no-one normal snored so blatantly.

She unlocked her ankles.

She must listen to her inner muse – find a solution before she was sent crazy.

5:11 a.m. Still awake – fretfully so – reliving thoughts and words she'd often thought, many she could not say aloud and, it now occurred to her as though it had never been otherwise.

Yet, family and friends often said how they always looked forward to receiving her postcards and letters, saying – often – they were like diary pieces.

Adding, she had a book inside herself...

He'd said, "And that's where it should stay."

Then it happened!

Eureka!

"Night shift," wherein, she would arise and write.

It was something she'd secretly wanted to do – but

too discouraged to do.

She closed her eyes and smiled defiantly...

Later on, she was surprised that she'd fallen into a contented sleep.

"After the storm..." she told herself, "nature resettles itself." So at 10:46 a.m., he was sent off, as usual, to meet up with his cronies at the bowling club.

Then, she cleared away the breakfast things, flicked the duster over anything upright, bed made, tide-mark on the bath tub removed and toilet bowl sanitised.

Exercised, feeling she'd wiped the slate clean, she brewed herself a fresh pot of tea before heading for the spare room.

To rearrange the dual bed back to a couch, set up the valet table and position the antiquity chair perilously close-by with the lidded commode accommodating a teas-maker plus stationary.

The basic needs.

Her bona-fide retreat.

Midnight could not come soon enough for her and, she was ready for it.

She closed the door leaving herself facing the landing staircase.

12:37 a.m. She folded back the cover of a new A4 notebook and, stared at the white blank page – thinking – a diary or a short story?

A diary, she reasoned, pen poised – only needed short, sharp, amusing and shameless golden nuggets of gossipy extracts so readers would appreciate enthusiasm and sarcasm.

Not like him.

He does everything loud – even his breathing...

She shuddered the image away.

Distraction was not an option.

She was on a mission and writing a short story first, could be the key to her independence.

She poured herself another cup of tea and savoured the choice.

Her choice.

She squirmed with delight.

A short story does deal in short time, and her story would be about someone or some others she knew.

Yes, she'd think of herself as a drama critic sitting on the front row, pen and note pad in hand.

After all, they'd never recognise themselves.

They never do by any stretch of their imagination.

Greedily she raised the teacup to her lips and drank noisily.

Pleasure, she mused, is a necessity of life and, pleasure had been and was scarce in her lifestyle.

She blotted the dribble from her hungry mouth – yes – she would turn perhaps into a certainty.

There should be no shame or blame attached to his inadequate pension causing them to live on a shoe-string budget.

She would relieve their predicament by becoming a freelance writer.

It was all the rage these days being self-taught. It shaped the mind.

She smiled distantly.

She would become her own woman.

The woman she'd secretly dared to dream to want to be...

She leaned in.

Her story would be a composition first – not a condensed novel – that would come later.

Meanwhile, if she found her exquisite words were too scarce to fill spaces and pages required, she would edit them with the precision of a ploughshare that cleaves to cold soil in autumn.

Then, take the advantage of the alternative route; a diary

A diary, she reasoned, would be more tell-tale and enable absurd entries which would be more fun.

Allowing her to be herself. More like her inner self.

She wriggled comfortably enjoying the sensation of risk-taking, being publicly known and talked about. Borne out of modest misery.

She detected nothing that needed to be avoided.

What could possibly go wrong?

She began to write, *The Invitation*:

The Invitation

I'm still recovering from yesterday's unexpected invitation to the opening of Avril Kelp's restaurant here in town.

She was an old school adversary.

She was always a brazen bitch, so I should have been on my toes, considering the place was full of people who didn't know each other – at least, didn't recognise one or the other with the passing of years.

The menu had the hallmark of herself – a gourmet chef, and so her menu was lathered in au fait language.

I found myself staring at the list of dishes with insane composure if only to acquaint myself – to guess the ingredients, and –

While I was guessing, the waitress – her daughter (she's beginning to look like her mother) – suggested the chef's special.

It was delicious.

I had two helpings.

When paying the bill, I congratulated Avril on the delicious meal I'd eaten.

Then inquired about the recipe.

Which I'd perceived as an exotic bird's egg – pouched – draped over a moreish cream sauce on lovely crisp wholemeal toasted bread.

She, the brazen bitch – smiled into my face; with arms akimbo, boldly said, she'd merely forked out the eye of a cod fish which included the attached optic nerve which gave the meal an extra flavour...

I wrenched!

Then coughed.

And coughed nauseously which shook my body into almost speechless exhaustion.

The unexpected old girls' reunion ended in unpalatable chaos.

DON'T COME BOTHERING ME

She stood in front of the lengthy mirror.
Admiring herself wearing a pricey dress.
It suited her colour of mood and eyes.
As though it had been styled for her.
Posturing naturally no guess.
Except for a seer's careful eyes.

She turned from her reflection.
Still wearing dress of high fashion.
Looking neither to right or left.
Turning on heel so much worn tread.
She headed for the exit door.

The store detective on alert.
Lengthened his stride to catch her up.
So the observer tripped him up.
To see her step through the out door.
Before he the lag with his spoils.
Unsuspected walked through the door.

THE END

Thank you for reading JAM TOMORROW
plus eleven more
Tales of the Unsuspected
volume 2

By the same author:
SAFE IN KILLER HANDS

Money, Madness, Murder

Revenge fiction – set within the four seasons of 1947

**"With the logic of betrayed,
the Asquith women instigate revenge –
murder dressed in its Sunday best"**

The Asquith women have been mastered, yet they are controlling together what they have been mastered by – Sam Asquith, land-owner. Found. Dead.

Sorrow turns to revenge when Stella Asquith – the vivacious widow – and her land-girl daughters, aided by their psychopathic farm-man, discover half-share of Sam's wealth has been bequeathed to a kept-in-the-dark illegitimate son.

Bitter in enmity, the murderous foursome instigate farming accidents which back-fire with dangerous risks and results. Killing Sam's son proves to be a deadly game of roulette.

SheAndTheCatsMother.com

About the author

It use to be said, you could recognise a Yorkshire person by the way they don't suck, they crunch a boiled sweet! Gwen Hullah, (maiden name), was born and bred in the West Riding of Yorkshire. Educated at Braithwaite School, Dacre, and Pateley Bridge Secondary Modern, Nidderdale. By tradition in those days, farmers' daughters became home-land-girls wherein horse-power ruled – as the saying goes – 'Shake a bridle over a Yorkshire man's grave and he'll rise up and steal your horse'.

Married for 28 years, Gwen resided in Grantham, Lincolnshire for most of those years. She became a free-lance writer, amidst other chance jobs – and the instigator of Radio Witham, Grantham Hospital Broadcasting Service in 1976.

Gwen has one daughter, Ida who is a musician singer/songwriter/guitarist (and author; pseudonym Zizzi Bonah) whom she's very proud of. They now live back home in Yorkshire with their variegated striped cat, Purrdey.

SheAndTheCatsMother.com